Praise for *Hagstone*

'*Hagstone* is a wonderful neo-mythic conjuration – soaring and delving into our dreams and fears'

MIKE MCCORMACK, author of *Solar Bones*

'A brilliant, gripping novel that explores the internal conflict of every artist – human relationships versus work; the urge to participate in society versus the urge to opt out'

SARA BAUME, author of *Seven Steeples*

'A beautiful, unsettling novel about the possibility of a woman crafting the shape of her own life, and the eternal connections we all have to the earth, sea and sky'

REBECCA TAMÁS, author of *Strangers*

'I loved *Hagstone* ... At the heart of this story is the disruption, solace, and affinity art-making offers, and this consoled and inspired me. A gift'

AMY KEY, author of *Arrangements in Blue*

'Gleeson's magnificent debut novel is that rare thing: a literary page-turner ... an entirely original tale that left me haunted and moved'

JENNIFER HIGGIE, author of *The Other Side*

'Exquisite ... A wildly seductive, gothic feminine tale of the sea, art, folklore, women, power and more'

KERRI NÍ DOCHARTAIGH, author of *Thin Places*

'Tense, mystical, and dark, *Hagstone* seems to arise from the natural world itself ... A deeply absorbing novel'

AMINA CAIN, author of *A Horse at Night*

'I read *Hagstone* with a feeling of ease and awe. Packed with the most incredible, sensuous nature writing; I felt I was living and breathing on that island'

JUNE CALDWELL, author of *Room Little Darker*

'A brilliant portrayal of the wild intensity of small island life ... I sometimes found myself holding my breath, as if under water, as I read this brilliant novel'

SALLY HUBAND, author of *Sea Bean*

ALSO BY SINÉAD GLEESON

Constellations: Reflections from Life

Hagstone

Sinéad Gleeson

4th ESTATE • *London*

4th Estate
An imprint of HarperCollins*Publishers*
1 London Bridge Street
London SE1 9GF

www.4thEstate.co.uk

HarperCollins*Publishers*
Macken House, 39/40 Mayor Street Upper
Dublin 1, D01 C9W8, Ireland

First published in Great Britain in 2024 by 4th Estate

1

Set in Stempel Garamond LT
Printed and bound in the UK using 100%
renewable electricity at CPI Group (UK) Ltd

For Colin, Claire and Daniel

'I hear those voices that will not be drowned'

– From Benjamin Britten's *Peter Grimes*,
as inscribed on Maggi Hambling's
sculpture, *Scallop* (2003)

Hagstone

Over townland and lake; over empty sheep dips and ancient walls. Past the old convent high on the cliff, where window frames gape like missing teeth. Past the deep reservoir, *drink, drink* and the forest fern fuzz. Soar over hangnail hills and long grass. To the dank forest of mulch floor and tree roots swollen like limbs uncovered in the earth. In the bay, boats bob like flocked birds. Above its stony crescent, a sturdy pier, and the lighthouse. The sea is steady for now. The land readies itself.

Back along the quiet, quiet roads full of blame, to that lovelorn cottage with the garden of herbs. Past the shit-matted coats of sheep, the long-vandalised phone box near the lighthouse tourists flock to, the pub with the walls glossed with years of paint. To the places they sometimes devoured each other.

Over a woman carving loops on viscous sand; and a man on a fishing boat, nauseous and lonesome. Over the dooms-day women singing in the sea.

Can you hear it?

Oh, Maman! Oh, Rathglas!

3

Over wildflower fields veined with ancient walls, tiny stone scars across the land. Over the rising sea and a woman carved into the rocks. Over pint drinkers slurp-gossiping. Over the people who never left.

Over the strange sound that taunts, spreading notes over the hills.

Over all the places to hide, to cede from the world.

Maybe that's why the Iníons came here.

PART ONE

1

Wave-fucked. That's how Nell describes the island. The cliff at Banshla rises up, a balustrade of shale. On the coldest days, the sea is the same colour, boiling around the base of the rock. Black water, white foam. From the far end of the strand, the headland resembles a woman from an old island myth.

Below the cliff face, waves froth the shore. Nell tips her bike onto the sand at Banshla beach, retrieving the camera and drone. Walking in concentric circles, marking a kind of solar system, she works her way along the beach, carving with a worn stick of driftwood. What would it be like to make this work somewhere else?

Whenever she imagines herself in another place, far from here, it's never in a city. Not a smog-belched place. No bridges spanning rivers like the vertebrae of some huge fish. It is always an island. More remote than this one. The kind of place survivors of a shipwreck wash up.

Catching fish, chasing crabs with cupped hands. Cooking at night by fire, a gold shadow on the sand. Everything black beyond a couple of metres. But the sea would be out there, the sound of the waves dancing in and out. Insects clicking in the trees, her salted mouth sucking the cooked fish from the bone.

She started a piece last summer at Dodder Bay. Carving lines and rings, endlessly scooping and digging into the gritty sand. Tearing around in her banger hatchback to make a perimeter. The whole thing came together in ten days, working from dawn until it grew dark. That summer, nearly eighteen hours of light fell on this coast. Long white panels of it, lighting up the water.

The impermanence of it was the appeal. It didn't matter if it disappeared, if someone kicked the sleek lines into blurred edges. The Banshla project will be bigger. She works in sections, figuring out the scale. There is something satisfying in feeling the sand, damp and velvet, part under the wood. To watch one line, so inconsequential on its own, become part of something else. It's hard work, so Nell takes a breather to change the drone's batteries. Sends it up to check the angles. A swim will help wake up the muscles. A dog appears out of nowhere, curious, ducking into rock pools.

It's September, and she tries to swim as late into the year as possible. By December, it's brutal, but today there's some heat in the sun. Always the way when the children go back to school. Nell strips to her swimsuit. Tucks the camera and drone under her jumper and begins the slow wade into the green swell, ice creeping up her legs.

The seabed slopes quickly, the pebbled surface gives way. Four metres from the shore feels like much further out.

Treading water, isobars of cold around limbs. Jellyfish are a frequent hazard. She saw a basking shark once, too close to the beach, and feared it would get dragged in by the current. Sometimes a curious seal appears, a slick head periscoping out of waves. She likes the company. Last summer there had been talk of a hammerhead shark.

Nell has swum in every nook and cove on the island, each with its own mood and temperature. Today's forecast promised clear skies, but it has begun to rain. Her favourite kind of swim, the tickle of drizzle on shoulders. Water on water. On her back, buoyant, looking up to meet the shower. Kicking; strong arms blading through the water. She won't last longer than fifteen minutes.

One last dive. Duck down, lung suck. The burble-burble in ears. Exhale and wait. The contractions of drowning. When she surfaces, a figure is moving along the shore, waving. Through the rain it's hard to tell if the hand is raised in warning or greeting. Curious, she swims faster, waves lifting each limb until the stones graze her knees.

The man is unfamiliar. Banshla, with its currents, isn't a beach that tourists favour. Immediately she worries for her camera and bag, but he just stands there, waiting for her to emerge. A rucksack hangs from one shoulder and he's carrying a fishing rod.

– You shouldn't swim here.

The tone is neither friendly nor concerned. It holds a kind of neutrality.

She waits, reluctant to offer an explanation.

– I've swum here for years, thanks. But am only really here for the sand.

She waves an arm in the direction of the morning's work.

– What about the sand?

The question seems genuine, although it's hard to miss the deep grooves she's made.

– Don't mind me. It's for a thing.

A flush of annoyance. For the inane comment and the diminishment of her own work. All the labour involved.

The towel flaps in the breeze. A discreet check on the camera. The bag is still closed. The underwear tucked underneath looks almost demure.

The stranger is tall. Striking, with a flintiness. Under one eye, the small pock of a scar. Noticing the stare, he adjusts his collar, self-conscious. What had he been doing on the beach before he saw her? Something moves across his face, a softening.

– Well, just be careful here.

He turns and heads back towards the road, kicking stones along the way. An uneven gait.

Cathal from the mini-mart, who she suspects wants to sleep with her, knows everything that goes on. She winds him up, calling him a nosy old lady, which he enjoys. Nell taps out a text, explaining the location, the scar. This is a face she'd definitely have remembered. She wants to know more. *Who is he?*

2

The morning at the beach passes too quickly, as it does when she's enjoying the work. The act of using her hands. Art was once Nell's full-time livelihood. Now it fits around making ends meet. But she isn't alone in this. Income is seasonal, and most islanders have more than one job. Relying on tourists from May to August when the ferry deposits them, green-faced after the twelve-hour trip, clutching cameras and swaddled in Aertex. Nell offers guided tours of the island – the lighthouse, the old well, splicing in the carving of Danu, the singing bridge, and supernatural elements like the sound. In summer, she'll take fifteen people paying a tenner each, gangs of Spanish students, families with bored kids, older couples who look more like siblings.

The tours happen late morning, to line up with the boats coming in. Nell waits for the groups by the anchor statue in the harbour. Today's gang are Canadians. They might get the jokes and understand her accent. Most want the tourist spiel, but occasionally someone thoughtfully asks what it's really like to live in a place like this. She'll joke about the unreliable broadband. Rail against the political corruption of the mainland council; the problematic water, even though the island gets rain upwards of three hundred days annually. The town has a predictable axis of buildings: a shop, a church, one pub. Abandoned houses with rotten gables. A lone, small hotel. The man who imports diesel also drives the school bus. The islanders rely on fishing, tourism, crafts. They share their skills, bartering to get a fan belt fixed. Food swaps too: carrots for cakes, fresh eggs for wool. There's only one doctor; he sells artisanal jam at the weekend market. The vet doubles as a midwife.

A man at the back asks about the weather. The sun, luke-warm in spring, edges a couple of degrees higher in summer. Autumn is brisk and bright, and winter seems to linger for two seasons. These days – even with new, bigger boats and sonar – there are fewer fish. Many have been lost at sea. It must appear to outsiders as a defiantly mundane place, but the group seem interested. Except for a young couple who would clearly rather be back at the hotel. The man, hand-some in a wolfish way, has his hand permanently glued to the woman's arse. Tall, pale, a hint of Viking about her blond plaits, protruding from an expensive branded hat.

While telling the group that there's only one place on the island where two cars can pass, Wolfman and Gudrun kiss passionately, whispering and giggling. It's enviable, their passion. Infectious too. Nell imagines herself and the man from the beach standing at the back of such a crowd on a tour. His mouth on her neck. But before the scene unfurls, she is back to her familiar monologue – *Barnakeel Bridge is nicknamed the singing bridge. The sea wind rushes through a hole in its parapet where its high note carries far and sounds like a woman singing. Locals say it's haunted.* (Tourists always *oooo* at this.)

Capitalising on their curiosity, she talks about shipwrecks and ghost sailors. Of twenty-two lives lost on the *Granuaile* seventy years ago, a real story she likes to embellish. Personal effects washed up for weeks afterwards. (True.) There are sailors' beds in several homes in the town. Hauled from the waves, each bearing a brass plate with a different number. (Also true.) Some wouldn't take them, thinking them cursed. They whispered that, if you did, a dead sailor would creep into your bedroom, sit on your chest, and vomit seawater into the sleeper's lungs. (Not true.)

In Nell's rewriting of the story, she tells the audience that the ship's crew became disoriented by the sound. Nor is the part where she blames the sound true. Not the singing bridge. The one that happens here and draws so many. On every tour someone asks about it. A phenomenon that plagues the island, with no warning or pattern. Some hear it, others can't. How it triggers other unexplained happenings. How it drives some mad.

In Nell's version, the captain on the *Granuaile* was tormented by the sound for two days until the ship foundered on rocks, the hull a twisted mess. She drops to a whisper, and predictably the tourists lean in, lapping it up.

The final stop is the old well. Crude stone steps lead down to a whitewashed wall hung with photos and votives.

Flickering candles light up lumps of moss. People come here to cure ailments: psoriasis, eczema, gut troubles. Nothing major, like claims of cancer cured, but the islanders believe the silvery water is sacred. Tourists always want to throw in coins, but Nell explains it's bad luck to mix paganism and capitalism. Instead, she hands out sprigs of lavender or rosemary from her garden.

The group queues up solemnly at the well and she tries to guess what each will ask for. Two women hang back, uninterested in the ritual. English. Londoners possibly, talking. Loudly discussing the price of their homes, whether it was madness to cram in another holiday before Christmas. Such a huge, chaotic place. Nell both loves and loathes cities. Full of people like these women, but also galleries, space, strangers. A kind of chaos she is sometimes in the mood for. Whenever these thoughts arrive, she takes it as a sign that she hasn't been off the island enough. But a holiday, even a cheap one, isn't an option.

Just as she is about to draw the tour to a close by handing out coupons for a free cup of tea at the Cove Inn, her phone pings. A reply from Cathal, relishing the feeling of being needed.

I'll find out who he is. Leave it with me.

3

Last year she'd been offered a residency in a warm country. It included accommodation in a villa, a pool, horses in a nearby paddock. The photos online showed a large mahogany desk overlooking a valley. A lemon tree outside the window. It was funded by a philanthropic family linked to greenwashing, so Nell turned it down. Whenever she allowed herself to think of it, it wasn't the art unmade, but that lemon tree, and the view, the absence of damp rocks and wind.

At home, after the tour, she peels off her damp things, soaked to her bra. The heavens had opened on the poor tourists in the end. On sodden days like this, wind gusting down the chimney, the thought of that lemon tree is enough to get her through the evening. She sets the fire with paper and sticks, a slab of turf, and coaxes it to life with a match. Every autumn at this turn in the year, the walls hold the cold more and it nudges a deep-rut feeling. The milk in the fridge is off, so she drinks black coffee, as she knows sleep will be elusive anyway. A mouse is moving behind the wall. What is its work tonight? Building a nest or just passing the unlit hours in kinship. Soon it will be another day of making things no one is waiting on. The elder tree outside creaks in the wind. The tree her mother hated. She wanted oak or ash, but there was no telling her father. As he dug in silence, her mother reminded him that elders were unlucky. Their wood should never be brought into a house. No one makes baby cradles from elder.

For a time, the old keeper's cottage beside the lighthouse had been a retreat for artists and writers. It was only a short walk away and Nell got the job of changing the sheets and collecting used linen. A handy side gig alongside the tours, and indoors, away from the weather. A chance to meet new people, until an accidental fire closed the place. The council have yet to refurbish it, but they pay Nell a small stipend to maintain the lighthouse. Discarding mice corpses and scraping gull shit off the walls. In summer, there was work to be had cleaning a scattering of beach bungalows. Washing towels, emptying bins. Dousing the rooms with air freshener because everyone ignored the no smoking signs.

It's hard to describe to outsiders what the isolation is like. It facilitates the life Nell has chosen, one possible because she has no ties or commitments. When the weather is fine in high season, the hotel puts tables outside. Sometimes, walking by on those summer nights, she feels the pang of it as she passes families, or gangs of friends, eating, laughing, at ease in each other's company. It catches her off guard. The conflict a surprise.

Nell had lost the bungalow-cleaning job after *the incident*. It had been a long summer of cloud cover, and boredom led to recklessness. The couple who saw her watching at their window had complained. Jimmy, the owner, was furious. Still, he regained enough composure to proposition her in exchange for a chance to keep hoovering the cheap carpets. Nell told him to fuck off.

It's tough, but possible, for her to live frugally. The cottage is modest. Three bedrooms, only one in use. The others are filled with boxes, bin liners of fabric, oars, a mildewy tent. Bags and bags of clay, industrial paint, latex, chicken wire. The sitting room doubles as a dining room. The oak table, piled with sketches and books, hasn't been cleared in years. She prefers to eat by the fire, plate on lap. The kitchen opens into the cottage garden and a plum tree that sags with polyps of fruit every September. In the vegetable patch, painstakingly coaxed over the years with much patience, she grows things to fill the gaps on the mini-mart shelves. Courgettes, tart cherry tomatoes, figs. Paddy from the ferry gave her wooden pallets to build a barrier to protect the herbs. Part of the land is ancient karst, and grikes in the stone shelter even the smallest plants. She longs to grow flowers. Delphiniums and waxy stargazers, but the wind is cruel to delicate stems.

Outside, darkness kneads the window as she pulls the curtains. The fire spits in the grate and she remembers that night, watching the couple at the beach cottage. Their perfunctory sex, yet she could not look away. Afterwards, the man showered, while the woman scrolled on her phone. She was beautiful, out of his league. Everything about this pair was a cliché. The expensive watch on the bedside locker. A Moët bottle. Famous, red-soled shoes.

It was a terrible job and she doesn't miss it, but it had routines. Without it, the clock means little. Drawing all night, forgetting to eat. She began making models of hands, but they were never quite right. Each had a different flaw. After making one hundred pairs, she lost it and didn't get out of bed for a fortnight. All or nothing, that's how it has always been. Ideas are not the problem. The cottage heaves with notebooks of false starts. Pages full of tiny shoots, untended.

In the kitchen, she crushes a fat clove of garlic, chops an onion, a handful of mushrooms. It all circles back to money in the end. Grimly filling out forms, hawking the work in funding drives. It feels gaudy to beg for help. Trying to explain in a series of boxes what a piece is about, when often it is only months later that she figures that out. Sometimes it's years, the components long packed away, or repurposed. It has stifled her. Commissions have dried up, emails have grown less frequent. Ten years ago, she could barely keep up with the invites. To New York, Melbourne, Bratislava. *I'm so busy*, she would bore on to friends. Occasionally, she misses that feeling. The full-glare attention. Until the reality drifts back. Bad hotels, scraping together change to buy a coffee at the airport. Currency and acclaim are both fleeting. All before she was even thirty. It is frightening – and fickle – how the interest in her work has waned. Her only option is to exist inside her art; outside of what anyone else is doing.

As oil warms in the pan, she realises there's no salt. The bread has gone mouldy. The day is draining away. Maybe she should take a trip. To a city on the mainland. One of those small boutique hotels, all dark velvet upholstery, with a tiny pretentious bar. She can almost taste the lightly poached eggs, maybe kippers, on an immaculate white plate. Anything to push away thoughts of the undeveloped, unfunded work. And how to survive the winter. Her appetite is gone. She throws the half-fried food in the bin and turns out the lights.

4

The island is always at its best at twilight. The baton passing of light between day and night. The harbour, rid of the daytime busyness, transformed into something enticing, as if about to spill a secret. The next evening, a tourist in Ryan's is buying rounds for everyone. He homes in quickly on Nell. Gauging her to be the only woman his age, with a gift for draining booze like the local hardened garglers. Beers, shots. Then Brandy Alexanders when the hour is late, and Johnnie wants to close up. It's the only cocktail he knows how to make, dumping massive shots of Bailey's and Cognac into pint glasses, without flourish. Later, back at his room, the tourist's seduction attempts are poor. Form addled by day-drinking that has run into night. Nell sits on the bed covered with a quilt of garish pink flowers. He kneels down and raises her shirt, clumsily stroking the skin, asking if he can kiss her 'tummy'.

– I'm not a fucking baby.

Nell feels the brandy climb back up her throat, pushes him away and stumbles out into the night.

On the way home, a text from Cathal. Reliable as ever.

That's _____ Cleary, but everyone just calls him by his surname. Been off island for donkeys' years. Only back a couple of weeks to look after a relative. Lives near the forest. That crappy little cottage with the red door.

It couldn't hurt to stroll up the hill. It's only a couple of miles and the air will do her good. Nell makes a feeble attempt at talking herself out of it, but the brandy urges her on. The night holds the first hint of winter. A face-stinging kind of cold. Nell moves through the trees, boots rustling through ferns. Tomorrow there will be a roux of metallic frost smeared on the grass. Twice, she considers turning back. The stupidity of it.

Trees stretch their limbs into the night, and in the gloam, two foxes are mating, their banshee howls shrill behind the thicket. It reminds her of an old installation she made in the forest on the Bean Sí. The folktale about a woman who shows up, singing, keening, to foretell a death. The whole project was a nightmare from start to finish. Time-consuming to pull together and then thwarted by bad weather. Looping wires around the trees, hoping branches would take the weight of the speakers. The possibility of electrocution. A journalist from the mainland wrote a review, declaring it 'moving'. This had irked her. The intention had not been to move. No matter how many times she walked around the installation, Nell couldn't understand why he'd said it. It was as if he'd reviewed a completely different piece. Her work was not meant to *move* people. All that she wanted, all that she asked of an audience was for them to be present, or curious. Maybe map it to their own experience. An artist friend remarked that the feminine – divine, supernatural, sexual – rattles people. The dead too.

About a week before it opened, when the speakers from Japan had arrived, in a very specific shade she insisted on, and all the leads had been checked, there was a moment. A fleeting minute when she didn't want to do it. It had been raining and she had worked too late, walking home, drenched and hungry, too tired to cook. A moment of plotting how to haul the speakers down to the post office hatch at the mini-mart and pay an exorbitant amount to send them back across two continents. Pack away all the extension leads and plugboards. Delete all the audio files. And just stop. Of course, she couldn't do that. It was a commission. Funded by a corporate sponsor who would come to the opening just to be photographed.

Sometimes at night, working on the banshee sounds, she had been disconcerted. Pacing the house, checking windows. Looking out at the raised beds and lavender clumps to make sure nothing was there.

The walk has taken longer than expected; skin hot under her coat by the time the cottage comes into view. Faded and asymmetric, she can just about make out walls covered in coloured slashes, as if someone has cleaned paintbrushes on the dashing. Smoke from a stove pipe rises steadily into the night.

Cleary is sitting at a table, some small tools lined up in front of him. A fishing rod, in pieces. To his left, a bottle of beer, glossy with condensation. Music is playing, filtering through the window in a jumble of notes. Hip-hop? Folk? Whatever he is doing looks like delicate work. Concentration spreads across his brow and she follows the line of his jaw, his lips. The way his hair falls over one eye. None of this was apparent on the beach, but he is unmistakably striking.

He is hunched over intently, attaching a metal float to a nylon line. In the middle of knotting it, he stops, consumed by some thought she will never know. What if the roles were reversed? She likes the idea of him standing at her window, watching. Has he thought about her since that day on the shore? Sleepy from the drinks, she makes her way back down the hill as a damp fog settles. Tonight, the International Space Station will pass over the island, moving through space and time above them, oblivious to this man fixing a rod, a dog barking in the distance, and in the hotel, a hand grasping someone's spine in pleasure.

5

The next morning, the bay tree by the front door is out of place. Only a couple of inches, exposing a dry crescent of concrete. An envelope tucked under the pot bears her name in a slanting, eloquent script. Someone has been here, and she didn't hear a thing. The thought unnerves her as she turns over the paper, handmade, rough. In the top corner is a woodcut symbol in green ink instead of a stamp. It's vaguely familiar. Like spotting an acquaintance's name in a newspaper article. She lifts the paper to her nose; it smells faintly of seaweed.

Dear Nell,
We hope the light of Danu shines on you. We write with an awareness and admiration of your art, and the skills that it attests to. It is our great wish to commission a work from you in relation to Rathglas (formerly St Brigid's convent).

If this is not of interest or you find yourself otherwise engaged, a refusal will not offend and we wish you a lifetime of fulfilment and peace, bathed in the light of our sister gods.

Yours,
Iníon Maman

Nell turns and steps back into the cottage, a little blind-sided. She places the letter on the mantelpiece and starts to clean out last night's ashes. There have been years of speculation about the women who live all the way out there, at the old convent. The letter contains no mention of money, but she's intrigued. Work is thin on the ground and winter, long and unforgiving on the island, is on its way.

At the end of the tours, people sometimes ask about the group. The locals call them 'the west island women', but they prefer to be known as the Iníons – a word from the old language that means 'the Daughters'. Before it was a convent, the building was the house of a wealthy family, now long gone. Tall, dark windows look down on to the bay.

Nell has always wondered how many live out there, but they keep to themselves so no one knows for sure. Women have been arriving on the ferry for some thirty years, bound for the big gates of Rathglas. That's what the group renamed it. As far as the islanders know, they do not consider themselves an organisation, or – despite murmurings on the mainland and some newspaper coverage – a cult.

From what she's heard, the women seem to come from all over the world, young and old. Some filter through the town en route to Rathglas, staying a night or two in the Cove Inn before taking the final leap. Most kept a low profile, but a handful talked to curious locals. Stories of ditching high-powered jobs and burnout. A number had extricated themselves from complicated families. Several washed up after catastrophic encounters with the spectrum of grief, including one whose ex-husband had killed both of their children before taking his own life. She'd heard a story from Babe Connolly, the island gossip, about two sisters who arrived together, both pregnant by the same man. Without judgement, they were shown to one of the larger rooms while the months passed until the birth of their children. One miscarried at sixteen weeks. The younger sister gave birth to a full-term stillborn son. The Iníons buried the infant in the small communal graveyard.

Babe likes to hold court at the mini-mart, giving Cathal all the latest gossip. Once when Nell went in to buy pegs, she was telling Billy who ran the boats and the two Lyons sisters that she'd been 'informed' that the women lived a simple existence. Given its gynocratic nature, Rathglas attracted activists and agitators, though you couldn't help but wonder if some were drawn here by the sound. From the varied tally Nell gleaned from Babe's updates, it was populated by ordinary women wanting a different kind of life.

She places the letter in the pile of bills on the table in the hall. It seems curious that they should reach out to her. And at this moment in time, when they have lived here so long and maintained such a stoic distance from everyone. What could they possibly want from her?

6

Every evening at Rathglas, the Iníons gather in the dining hall. The room is warmed by a large range that emits a comforting kind of heat. The gatherings on the long benches are a wind-down. A vow of silence is not obligatory, but many spend their days working in quiet contemplation. They welcome the chance to eat together and talk about practical things: schedules for laundry and cooking, the assignment of chores.

Iníon Ebele moves about the hall lighting lamps. A ship's horn sounds on the horizon, a reminder of the world still turning, far from their seclusion. No one is asked about life before Rathglas, or their reason for coming here. This culture of discretion has led to the creation of an outlet: a weekly evening assembly. Put together by Iníon Rose, after much negotiation with Maman. Every Wednesday, like today, the women are invited to submit single words for discussion after dinner; passed forward on slips of paper to be placed in an old teapot. The subjects tend to be broad. They've previously covered class, euthanasia, the afterlife. When the assembly night had not been running for long, Maman suggested a veto system. A recent discussion on art turned out to be one of the more engaging evenings, veering towards the bad men of art. Gauguin's paedophilia. Picasso's treatment of women, who he called 'machines for suffering'. Iníon Aisling talked about Surrealism. How everyone references Dalí, but Leonora Carrington and Dorothea Tanning were superior in every way. She spoke in hurried sentences about symbolism and the deconstruction of shape. The other Iníons often found her intimidating, but she also had a way of drawing everyone in. She seemed to hear things before anyone else. The first to know about new rules and who was sick. Whether she was slopping out pigs or hanging out laundry, she sang all the time.

Rose fishes a scrap from the teapot.

– Tonight's word, sisters, is 'FEAR'. As ever, there is absolutely zero obligation for anyone to contribute. Raise your hand if you'd like to speak, and don't talk over your fellow Iníons. Who'd like to get us started?

The room is quiet, as is usual at the start of the evening. It isn't that the Iníons have nothing to say, but rather that they don't want to be seen to be first. It might appear too eager to hear the sound of one's own voice. Maman often chastises them, emphasising the egalitarian nature of Rathglas, that they are here to leave pride to the outside world. She discourages them from gathering in each other's rooms for frivolous conversation. But a night spent like this is a marker against solitude. Against cold corridors and the wind whistling through gaps in the old skirting boards. Some speak even if they haven't much to say, just to feel

connected. For one or two of the quieter Iníons, these will
be the only words they'll speak all week. That's the way
of it here.

Rose sits up a little straighter, tucking a curl back under
her headscarf. She often starts proceedings and rumours
have spread – because of the degree of her involvement –
that she rigs the topics.

– OK, I'll get the ball roll—

Just as she speaks, Iníon Sile volunteers. Rose hides her
annoyance.

– Thank you, Sister, go on.

The old radiators hiss. Iníon Z takes out her knitting. Sile
clears her throat.

– My old life was … fine, to be honest. Couldn't
complain. But deep down, I had this feeling. A gutful of
longing for something. I wanted to feel a sense of security
that I never did out there. And I *do* feel that here. I guess
I used to feel scared a lot.

The women murmur assent. Ebele waits, tempering the
frown that is forming. Outgoing and no-nonsense, she
stays out of discussions about kitchen duties or desalina-
tion tubs but lives for the assembly night. The chance to
joust, think, hear how other people's minds work. She leans
in to the conflict, not out of malice, but for fear that the
Iníons might lose their curiosity. Living in such close prox-
imity can lead to familiarity and conformity. It would feel
remiss not to remind the Iníons that they could and should
disagree. There is a particular joy to be had in lobbing an

incendiary remark just to watch the shock, the bomb radius spreading through the group.

– To whatever mystery person chose this word, I salute you.

Ebele looks pointedly at Rose, who opens her mouth to speak, but Ebele presses on.

– My question is this – what's the point in feeling scared?

A door bangs and the cook, Iníon Sadhbh, bustles in with an old trolley. Spoons rattle on saucers and the Iníons pass around their cups of hot, stewed tea.

– To clarify, Ebele, no one is saying it's wrong to feel afraid sometimes. It's primal, and there's no way to control it. I accept Sile's point – and I'm only speaking for myself here – but it's unhealthy to live in a state of perma-terror.

– 'Perma-terror?' Oh god. Is that not a bit much, Rose?

Ebele salts the wound further by using quotation fingers.

Spoons are frantically stirred. The Burko boiler wheezes on.

– No one – here in Rathglas – should feel afraid? Sure, you can barely get into the place …

This is Iníon Muireann, the most laid-back of the group, liked by all.

Rose bristles, forcing a smile.

– We've all known fear. In the past, I mean. Before we came here.

– But being afraid is a waste of time, Rose. You absorb it. I know I have.

Ebele isn't going to let this go but Rose is happy to pivot from debater to moderator, changing tack to officiousness when it suits.

– If I could just remind the group about tone. And being civil? These conversations are for everyone. We should be mindful of how we respond to the lived experience of others …

– You know that's not what I'm talking about, Rose.

Silence. A cough. Z's knitting needles click like bones. Arguments like this at evening assembly are rare but, despite the shared ethos, not all opinions overlap. Some of the clashes arise out of boredom. For Ebele a spark of conflict makes her heart thump, sets the blood charging in her veins. But it comes from anger too. She knows that. A past weight never fully discarded.

Z puts her hand up.

– I once knew this woman who was married to a terrible man. He used to beat the hell out of her and their kids. Spent all their money on horses and pints. Lost his job, got angrier, drank every day. For a long time, she never slept more than an hour or two a night. Certain he'd murder her in her sleep. Soon, she couldn't actually remember what it was like to *not* feel afraid. She told me the fear kept her on her toes, you know, in a state of hypervigilance. She learned to fold into her life. It made me sad. But mostly furious.

– No one is saying that fear is something you have to adapt into your life.

This is Rose again, determined to keep control of the conversation.

– I wasn't finished.

Rose is sorry she started this.

– But what happened, Z? She just accepted her life and got on with things?

– No. Not at all, actually …

– So, what did she do?

– She won the lottery and left the fucker.

A murmur of laughter rises, abating the tension.

– And I'm not telling you this story to make light of tonight's word, but I prefer when the topic doesn't get so dark.

Rose nods at Z, relieved that a row had been averted.

Sadhbh claps her hands in a schoolteacher-ish manner.

– Sisters! Maybe tonight's topic was a little too … much. Now, if you don't mind, I have cups to wash and would appreciate you all calling it a night.

Maman, who has been sitting a few rows back, leaves the room quietly.

The Iníons begin to disperse, piling cups onto the trolley, murmuring good night. Muireann lingers by the window and asks some of the others to stay, while Rose packs away the old teapot.

– I heard something odd about Samhain. Did anyone else?

Muireann leans in to the group. Sile and Aisling exchange a look.

– I did too – that Maman is planning to commission something for this year's ceremony.

This is Iníon Aurora, who's been quiet all night.

– What's that all about?

Ebele speaks, less combative than earlier.

Sadhbh bustles back in from the kitchen, interrupting.

– Yes, from an artist who will be coming to stay for a while. I delivered the letter to her myself.

Sadhbh does not know if this is true but enjoys the looks on their faces as she shunts them out into the hall.

As Muireann makes her way up the stairs to the dorm, she wonders why there had been no discussion in advance with the Iníons, especially at evening assembly. Maman had been there, at the back of the room, but had not said a word all night.

7

Banshla is deserted this morning, save for the birds. Two large gulls are engaged in a tug of war over mackerel innards. The speckled one is victorious, sweeping towards the cliff to eat the spoils. The strand is deserted, and Nell considers skinny-dipping. Plunging right in, offering her skin and bones to the waves. Too many bored teenage lads on the island have drones, so it would be a risk. The water is cold as a fjord. She lasts ten minutes, before crawling back out. The gulls have moved to the end of the beach with the rest of the flock, squawking over the feast of a seal carcass. Nell knows another artist who told her she wanted a Tibetan Sky Burial. To have her corpse cut up and left to be eaten by vultures.

Nell has still not replied to the letter. Torn, because an idea for a project is forming. Just fragments, but this is always the time to let it sit. If she says yes to the Iníons, it will have to wait. The irony of postponing a durational piece about the concept of time passing. Living in the lighthouse for a week, staying awake and upright during the hours of darkness. Inside the lantern room, making herself into a silhouette that could be seen all over the island, a different colour gel filter over the beacon for every night, up behind the glass. Her body and the light, refracting through the plastic film. Beaming a silhouette of herself out on to the ocean. The council will have to be convinced that nothing will interfere with the function of the beam, or the safety of those out at sea. She would be free to work on it now. A rejection for a residency on the mainland arrived this morning. She'll look at the other letter again later.

Moving across the shingle, she eyes the clouds, clutching rain in their grey bellies.

The waves are white tulle and she walks – *1-2, 1-2* – heart keeping time with her strides. Last time, Cleary was here, but now there is no one around. She could pay him a visit later, hover at the window. As she is weighing this up, the gulls take off, quick as applause. One calls out, another joins in, forming a maudlin chorus. She hears the first familiar note of the sound that haunts the island. A murmur one might mistake for the sound of a party drifting through a wall, a sub-woofer in a boy racer's car. The beat-up generator out the back of Ryan's. Everyone has their own way of describing it. Best to get off the beach and seek shelter. Nell runs, pushing heels into sand and *run, run.*

She soon reaches the track that leads off the beach and ducks into the old changing rooms. Heartbeat asymmetric, breath short, listening to the sound bouncing off the corrugated roof. The wail of the birds stops suddenly, followed by the sound itself coming in. A tinny thud close above.

Then another, and another. The windows are ceiling-high; she can only imagine the scene outside.

The birds keep dropping for several minutes. The roof is horribly dented and Nell fears it might cave in. When the noises finally stop, she opens the door. Outside, twenty or so of the poor creatures are scattered on the ground. Mostly gulls. Some unscathed, almost peaceful. Others utterly mangled. Twisted legs, eyes scooped out on impact, a blizzard of feathers. The smell of death mixed with seawater. A lone gannet, twisted and bloody, lies broken in the basket of her bike.

8

At home, she is shaken. Craving comfort, she takes a chicken from the chest freezer for dinner. On rare Sundays as a child, they'd have a roast, her father frying mushrooms and onions in cream, thinking it fancy. The kitchen would fill with delicious flavours, her mouth a tiny well. He'd present the dish, doing a bad French accent that made her squeal with laughter. It was the only time she remembered the feeling around the table as warm and secure. Home could feel like the safest place in the world, and other times the opposite. Nell wonders about the women in the old convent. Their lives before they came here. If their need for isolation is linked to the changing earth or the climate, a red-letter word for any island dweller. And do they hear the sound? While the oven warms, she examines the letter again.

It is our great wish to commission a work from you.

Whenever she's applied for residencies or bursaries, she's always hated the long-finger response. It has taught her to reply quickly. *Yes, no, is it paid?* How do they know about her?

The urge to resist is there, but the obvious thing is to say yes. Curiosity and money are good motivators. It would mean company too, conversation, and she is perhaps too used to solitude. The longer she lives alone, the harder it is to reintegrate. A sizeable number of islanders are single dwellers, especially the part-timers. Here for fishing work, leaving families behind on the mainland. Nell often runs through an array of bleak scenarios. If she were to fall ill or collapse it could take days or weeks to be found. Not until the rats had had a go. In the dregs of winter, she had watched a TV programme about the people who clean up dead bodies that have gone long undiscovered. Traipsing around pitiful flats in white forensic suits. The really graphic bits were blurred out and yet Nell squinted at the screen, wanting to see. One cleaner, voice muffled behind a mask, said something that she's never forgotten.

'*By the time we find some of them, they're mostly liquid. Congealed. Getting the stains off the floor is the hardest part.*'

Liquification. There is something comforting in it. A final, ruddy relinquishing. It sounds more appealing than morose fragments of grey ash.

Saying yes would also be an antidote to boredom. The lighthouse project would be kicked down the road, but the sense of wanting to know is strong. To learn more about these women who live outside parameters the world was desperate to impose on them.

There have been predictable rumours. That they are a coven or some sort of prepper cult. Living a solitary existence is not proof of either, but lack of contact with the islanders had fuelled this line of thinking. Dr Foran is the only local to have been inside the walls, when a young Iníon nearly died of a burst appendix. Babe Connolly's intel said the women gifted him a basket of apples and a handmade blanket in gratitude. They always send the same woman into the town on the rare occasion they need something in an emergency. The Iníons, as far as the islanders know, possess no black-hearted aversion and bear them no hostility.

Rathglas is their world and now they are inviting her in. A summoning, maybe.

Who was it who wrote that islands by their very definition beg the question of beginnings? Maybe this is the way to look at it.

She will hear them out.

9

In a remote place, desire is complicated. Everyone in their twenties from here to New York just wants to drink, party, fuck. Nell, a decade on, sees this part of her life is heading for the rear-view mirror. Memories of parties in the island's forest that went on all weekend. A rollover of pills and lighting cigarettes the wrong way round. Dancing for six hours, feeling the bass jump in her body. A steady stream of hungry men. Grappling against silver-coated trees. The rising sun glinting through branches as she lay under someone, rutting amid the leaves. *Oh, those days.* The flipside for others meant that a small pool of people led to unreciprocated lust and frustration.

That night, outside Cleary's, she wonders which of the local women he's been with. Who was his first? How many? She's been with a lot of island men. On the beach, in damp bedrooms. Their lives don't interest her. Their hopes or habits, the things they want. But each has told her things. Who owed money, who liked booze too much. Which women wouldn't allow their husbands to touch them. She feels pity. Disdain too, that they can't find a way out of that lack of connection. Every time she's on top of someone, or men have leaned in, climbing her body like a cliff, she feels a pang for their unfuckedness.

Cleary's curtains are open, or maybe there aren't any, given the perfunctory state of the dwelling. All heat from the stove lost through the glass. He's burning through logs at some rate. *Idiot.* On the table are colour gel filters, the kind some local lads use on lamps when hunting hares. This presents a possible, unexpected conversation opener.

Hello, I've been gawping in your window unbeknownst to you, but HEY, could I have some of those gel filters for an art project in a lighthouse? TY.

Each night something new about him reveals itself. The accelerated blink rate, as if trying to understand something cryptic. The angle of his nose. Roman? Aquiline. His stubble, a scouring of black points on his chin. Eyes closed, she imagines it brushing her lips, her face, her thighs. An image of teenage hunger and beard rash. A petroleum scald in the groin.

Cleary opens a beer. A *ciotóg*. Left-handed. Something they used to try and beat out of kids in the local school. The room is sparse. A boxy television, a shelf with a handful of what look like manuals or maps. By the fire, underwear and a woollen jumper cling to a lopsided clotheshorse. She experiences a sudden and inexplicable sadness. Not for him, or about him. But for herself. That, despite the accumulation of years, life isn't where it could be. The fact that she always feels the right answer is just out of reach. The moon flickers behind the clouds, a silver plate looming.

Would he be disgusted or turned on by this lurking? He
might even be impressed at the discipline, the commitment.
Distracted, she steps back, sensing the misstep too late.
Connecting with the recycled empties by the back door.
The sound like a klaxon.

Shit!

He turns quickly, alert, listening. By the time he's up out
of the chair, Nell is gone.

Years from now, she imagines herself visiting an expensive therapist in a city far from here. Sitting in an elegant
red-brick house on a tree-lined street. Actual art, not print
reproductions framed on mallard green walls. A single delicate orchid in a pot in the hall.

*Did you think – deep down – that you wanted to be
caught?*

Of course not, she would reply. *I didn't want him to
think I was a fucking degenerate.*

Well, maybe just a bit …

10

Nell's cottage is south of the old convent, which is on the westerly, most remote side of the island. Greenawn beach is a striated mix of sand and shingle at the end of a long curving road. In some light, it looks as if the sea has climbed all the way up to the bike railings, but it's the blue of mussel shells, butterflied and spent. The bay is surrounded by hills, incubated. The route up to Rathglas is more track than road. Grass and ancient hedgerow ooze outwards to meet a central grass strip running the length of it. The ditches heave with clover and bloody cranesbill; devil's bit scabious in blue and violet, sturdy oxeye daisies. She left early, hoping there'd be no one out, and is glad of the bike, push-pushing on the pedals, leaning into the incline. The island hills are as familiar as the bones of her own body. What she expends on the exhausting slow climbs, she makes up for on the freewheel down. Dawn creeps nearer, the sky splashed with pink. A lingering indigo gives way to the day. She was meant to give a tour to a group of Croatians this morning. The money would have been helpful. The tips too.

Further up the steep track, she longs for the gates to appear around every bend, but there are only more hedgerows. An occasional hawthorn, a curious cow sticking its head over a gate. The island graveyard is a little further, a place she finds peaceful. The same cluster of surnames. Imposing etched crosses. Different lives buried with the same view of the sea for eternity.

Cleary windmills through these thoughts. A flicker of lust ripples through her as she stops to pick red clover. Pulling out each flowerhead, examining the white chevron pattern. As kids, they sucked the nectar at the end of the stem for a sugary hit. Overhead, bulbous clouds move slowly. Up here, a high view of the harbour as a boat spills its catch on the dock. The gulls descend, shrieking. Two years ago, she made a durational piece about the tides over twenty-four hours. Finite and then gone forever. The audience ignored the no-phones instruction. Clips of the water appeared online in minutes, contradicting the ephemeral nature of the whole thing. Once a work is out in the world, there's no way to control the responses. It was too much to ask people to immerse themselves. To be present. *Put the fucking cameras away!* she'd shouted.

That was past. The present is, or could be the lighthouse installation, or the land piece at Banshla. The notebook by her bed is full of writing that by morning is illegible. Turning on the light sends inspiration scuttling into the dark like an animal. All she can hope is that there might be a new idea at the end of this track. Around one last corner and there it is: the gates of Rathglas. A place she has longed to see.

11

The gate to Rathglas has a buzzer. Nell half-expected a campanile with a brass bell. Or a requirement to rattle the frames to announce her arrival. The reality is disappointingly standard. An off-white button, emitting a jarring tone. There is still time to back out, to not ignore the anticipatory rumble of new work. But it's true that a general stasis has set in. This change of scene might help.

The convent isn't visible from the road. The gate opens with a mechanical shudder, hinges squealing. No one comes to greet her, so Nell walks up the sloping drive, past ash, beech and a lone magnificent Scots pine tree, towering and resolute. The air and trees are still, but below, the sea makes its presence known. In the distance, a sibilant swell rises up every now and then. There are few places on the island where the waves can't be heard.

And suddenly there it is. It doesn't resemble a place of retreat, or even a convent. It's clear it was once a very grand building, projecting a sad, stately quality, like a crumbling mansion in a period drama. Part of the roof is shaped in boxy battlements. Being around old buildings always makes Nell pensive. The weight of the past, pushing through the stone. The ghosts of each person who lived or died there. Palpable and proximate.

She is so engrossed in taking in the building that she doesn't notice someone approaching. Assertive steps crunching on gravel. A woman, wide-hipped and intent, raises an arm in welcome. Nell grips the outstretched hand.

– I'm Iníon Aisling. Welcome to Rathglas.

– Thank you. Glad to be here.

She is clutching a hammer, which alarms Nell slightly.

– Not for me, I hope?

Aisling laughs.

– No, I'm fixing something. I hate not being busy. Idle hands and all that. So – you got Maman's invitation?

– I did. Am very curious, I have to say.

– Such a long way, no? I haven't done it in years, but still remember my first time. Huffing and puffing past each bend and wondering how much further it was.

Nell wants to say that this was her exact thought and ask if the other women who came here felt that too, but it feels wrong to be overly familiar from the off. She sees a figure at one of the upper windows watching before turning away.

After the greeting, Aisling is quiet as they move up the path to the building. An impressive door is ajar, and Nell follows her into a gloomy vaulted hall. It feels colder than the air outside, their feet echoing.

– Wait here. I'll let Maman know you've arrived.

The deference is surprising. That there would be hierarchies here when its reputation suggested it was an egalitarian enclave. But then again, someone is always needed to steer any ship. The quiet of the hall suddenly makes it feel all the more isolated. A little unlived in too, as pockets of large, old buildings often are.

A young woman, no more than nineteen or twenty, appears through another door.

– *Suaimhneas.* I'm Iníon Sile. Please follow me.

The girl is slight, a thinness enhanced by the pale shock of her face. They turn off the hallway and pass an open door where three women are meditating, or praying. Light floods over the floorboards, picking out floating dust. Nell wishes the panes were lower, to see the view from up here. They continue into an older part of the building and up a bare, narrow staircase. The windows overlook a well-tended garden of apple and plum trees, raised beds of vegetables. A stone well, various outhouses and sheds.

She is about to ask how much further, when the woman stops abruptly and knocks at a door.

– Come in.

They step into a large light-filled room. The carpet is worn but soft and a hefty desk sits near one of the windows. Beside it, a large globe of the world, set in a mahogany cradle. On one wall, unexpectedly, a plain, unframed mirror. Nell turns at the sound of a familiar noise, mechanical, repetitive. An older woman is pedalling away on an exercise bike, an ancient, clunky model. Bemused, Nell waits as she executes a tricky dismount, thanks to a long smock.

– Please forgive me. I'm a firm believer in routine and I do this every day at the same time. Five kilometres without fail. It's so important to keep the body strong as well as the mind, don't you think? It's Nell, isn't it? You are most welcome to Rathglas. We weren't sure you were coming when we didn't hear from you.

She dabs at her brow, her face neutral.

– I wasn't entirely sure how to get in touch, and figured I'd just come out here – but maybe it's a bad time?

– Not at all. Thank you so much, Sile, you may go. Sit down, Ms—

– Nell is fine.

– Well, thank you, Nell. We are grateful that you've come to see us – and not without a great deal of curiosity, I am sure. I'm Maman.

The woman doesn't offer her hand and retreats to the desk, indicating instead that Nell should sit in the chair opposite. The accent is not local. Hard to place, a mix of capsized vowels and hard consonants, as though she's lived in many places. Studiously clipped and shaped to create a demonstrative kind of authority.

– I'm truly honoured that an artist of your stature would even consider this commission. It means a lot to me and the other Iníons. No doubt people in the town talk, but I can assure you we're very ordinary.

She manages a tight mask of a smile, moving a paper-weight from left to right, straightening a notebook and pen.

Nell's own uncloistered life has often been erratic, hand-to-mouth. Devoid of the discipline and order that must go on here. She is curious and finds it hard to judge them. If anything, that kind of steadfastness is rare in a fickle world. Conscious of overstepping, she treads carefully.

– To be honest, it doesn't take much to get their tongues wagging. Most people only relate to one way of living. Their own way. They don't understand – or even try to understand – anything else.

Nell knows this suspicion is directed as much at her as the Iníons. At the docks buying fish one morning, she was stuck behind the Lyons sisters in the queue. Two bigger mouths you'd be hard pushed to find. Wide-eyed niceties to people's faces, but their schtick was to lob question after question. Whatever this yielded would later be casually dropped into salacious chats in the mini-mart. The younger sister, possessed of fine hair and the more forked tongue of the two, asked Nell what kept her occupied in the winter months. Nell explained that she was an artist, to which Lyons the Elder responded tartly: 'And how do you make money from that?' Her sister, angular, vulture-faced, pushed on, demanding to know how exactly she got by. Bristling, Nell took the parcel of sole from Davey, spun around and announced: 'Oh, I supplement my income by sleeping with your husbands.' It was worth it. And she *had* slept with one of their spouses, before he was married.

– Would you mind if I asked, what made you all come here?

Maman is calm, ready for the question.

– We came here seeking refuge nearly thirty years ago. Myself … I feel – very strongly in fact – that I was summoned here. Something called me. I felt it the moment I saw Danu from the boat, that she was part of it. Since then, women continue to arrive at our door – I'm guessing that the world hasn't gotten any better.

– But why this place? The world's full of islands and there's no shortage of remote hideouts.

– Ah, but we are not hiding.

Her eyes twinkle.

– What is it you do out here, I'm genuinely curious.

– There's honestly not much to it. We choose to reject the world outside with all its hatred and inequality. All things that make an already hard existence harder. So we live a very simple life of gratitude and community. That's it.

Nell takes the glass of water Maman offers. The woman watches her closely. This might be the last possible moment she can decline. Walk back out the gate.

– The work we do matters. We've never turned anyone away, even when food is scarce.

She trails off.

– I imagine you had made your own assumptions about us before you got here?

– Not really … but I'm sort of fascinated by Rathglas, I guess that's why I'm here.

Maman takes a sip of water. It is difficult to gauge her age.

– What I want … is for people to know what we did here – what we actually *do* here. To counter all the stories. That's why I had the idea of writing our history.

– But what does this have to do with me?

– I can't write it. Nor can anyone here. It needs an outsider's eyes. Some distance. We want *you* to tell our story.

Whatever Nell might have been expecting, this wasn't it. The first thought forming in her gut is to say no. Projects like this can get complicated.

– I've written a little in the past – catalogue essays for other artists, text pieces for installations – but I don't think of myself as a writer. I don't call myself one. I'm definitely more of an artist.

– But you've written about other women, and women not unlike us, haven't you?

Nell is confused, her mind flips back through past projects.

– A woman came to us four, maybe five years ago. She didn't bring much but was adamant about hanging on to a handful of books, including a small, well-thumbed volume on Biddy Early.

Nell is surprised. The project was a one-off but meant a lot to her. She was approached to work with a group of local artists for an arts centre on the mainland. Each person was asked to make a small book commemorating a woman in history who had been mistreated but whose reputation had endured. Biddy Early, a gifted herbalist who was rumoured to be a witch, was an obvious choice for Nell. It was amazing no one else thought of her. Biddy was famous for potions and curing people but was accused of witchcraft. Nell made her own pastes from the garden, or whatever the sea offered up, and felt kindred. The budget for the project had been minute and it was hard to do the story justice, but she cared deeply about it. It was a small act of redivivus. She was touched by how many young women got in touch afterwards. Biddy was the figurehead they were searching for. Independent, altruistic, supernatural. At one reading, a devotee proudly showed off a full-sleeve Biddy tattoo.

– And there was your female bible.

Maman has done her homework. Nell's face gives her away.

– Don't assume we're oblivious to what goes on outside of here …

The realisation is swift, despite the amnesiac patch in her brain.

– Oh god. I actually sent you one.

– You sent *us* one.

– I just assumed it wouldn't get through, let alone that anyone would read it.

– We do receive post. Mr Kenny is very respectful of our privacy. Rings the buzzer, leaves any letters we get at the door in a plastic bag. We all read your bible, passed it around for weeks. Our library isn't frequently replenished, but we pride ourselves on what's there.

Nell glances at the bookshelves to her right, half-expecting to find it there, and it is very clear that saying no is not an option.

– Well, like I say, I'm not exactly a writer.

– That's precisely why we thought of you. What I have in mind is something looser, less definitive. Maybe with some manner of imagery or illustrations, but you'd know best. A small commemorative work that shows who we are, and what we have strived to do.

Nell has always wanted to know more about the Iníons. And on a practical level, this time of year is the pits for work. A season of hibernation and early nights instead of lighting the fire. Deep down she knows it is the wrong time for the spiral project, or most outdoor work for that matter. From here until Christmas the weather will only worsen.

– How would it work?

– Any way you want it to, but the root and branch of the story is the women. When people arrive, they give a personal account of themselves and why they've come. Testimonies, in a way. You're welcome to use them.

– And it would be OK for me to read that stuff?

Maman stares. A strange hesitance. The way Nell's father would pause when furious but holding his tongue.

– This book is for the greater good of us all. Of course they won't mind.

– Would you need me to be based here or at home? I don't want to get in the way.

– Both. You can come and go as you please, but it would be helpful if you spent some time here to experience Rathglas. See how we live, meet the Iníons.

In another life, Nell thinks she might have come here too. Receding from the world with its grief and inequalities and responsibilities, the hard graft of trying to keep it all afloat.

Maman waits for a response.

– When do you need it by? The project.

– Ideally, Samhain. We hold a ceremony every first of November. This year is our thirtieth anniversary and it's important to me that we do something a bit special. You know, make an occasion of it for everyone.

– I'm still not convinced I'm the right person for this, but I could take a look at the archive and see if it's something I can do?

– We hope you will, Nell.

Maman beams. The smile is intended as beatific but doesn't quite come off. They know and respect her work and this, possibly because it is meant to, flatters her.

– If nothing else, you'll get to meet many interesting people. How about jumping right in? I'm sure you'd like to get a feel for the place?

Maman rings a bell and the young, pale woman reappears.

– Sile, we'll take tea in the cliff garden shortly. Thank you. Come, Nell. I'll show you around.

12

Instead of returning the way they'd come, Maman moves
to the other end of the corridor and opens an old fire exit
door out to the side of the building. The air is welcome
after the stuffiness of the office. They descend the metal
stairs, attracting the attention of a handful of women in
the garden, dressed in smocks of the same dark shade.
Two are taking sheets off a washing line, coming together
in a dance to fold them. Several others are working, weed-
ing, and hoeing. A woman in a headwrap tips peelings
into a trough for some sturdy pigs who lap it up, ears
flapping. Large greenhouses stretch back behind them.
There are rows of seedlings waiting to be put in the
ground. Wheelbarrows, barrels half-filled with rainwater.
Spades lined up against a potting shed wall. Outbuildings
in various states of repair are spread around the perimeter, and there is a small, ancient-looking chapel, sitting
perilously close to the cliff edge. Against all this, the
dominant background is the sea, omniscient and azure, a
spangled mass. A noise, raucous and unexpected, draws
Nell's gaze to chickens racing up and down a run behind
the shed.

– In the small field beyond the chickens, we have cows, goats, a couple of sheep and an elderly horse.

She pauses, raising her hand, beckoning someone behind Nell.

– Just so you know – we don't eat horses.

The woman who's been feeding the pigs waves back and Maman opens an iron gate and bids Nell follow her. The path is narrow, so they walk single file, leading to a garden of flowers and shrubs. Clematis shouldn't survive the wind up here, but there it is, pushing its cream flowers out showily. Honeysuckle clings stubbornly to a wall. Gold marigolds, alliums, red fists of peonies, and miraculously, sunflowers. Maman follows her astonished eye.

– Muireann has green arms, never mind green fingers. She can grow anything.

They sit at a table. Sile appears again with cups, a pot of tea and a plate of cake cut into treacly slabs. The sun makes a valiant effort to inch higher. The mainland is half a day from here, but the neighbouring rocky outcrops are visible. Nell has her own names for these rocks – words for water or weather – in the native language. There are caves below, the water rushing in and out sounds like the boom of a cannon. She has never taken on anything like this but is trying to assess if it might bring something new to her own practice. Nell wants to understand them and their spartan existence: what do they get from it? Is it enough? If she accepts the commission, the answer may come – or she will at least have earned their trust enough to ask outright.

Two Iníons nearby whisper and beckon to another across the garden. Nell turns to Maman.

– Is there anything I should know in advance?

– We're fairly open here, which probably sounds like a contradiction, but we have a trusting community. As you're not an Iníon, you're not bound by the same code, but we expect a basic decency – and respect for the way we live. We hold our privacy very dearly, so we'd appreciate your discretion in keeping your work, what you see or hear, to yourself.

All at once, Nell finds she is keen to get to work. Not knowing where to start with a project, or where it might end up, always brings a mixture of nerves and uncertainty.

– We've set up one of the rooms as a studio. I've asked Muireann to leave some folders there for you, but I'm sure you'll have plenty of your own ideas.

A desk. A studio. The dawning realisation that they already knew she'd accept.

– And Samhain is the deadline?

– For the moment, take your time. Get your bearings with it, but yes, that's the date we have in mind. Now, I must run. Sile will show you where the studio is. Good day, Nell. *Suaimhneas.*

As Maman leaves, Nell notices an elderly woman in a wheelchair by one of the sheds. A blanket is tucked around her knees and her hands bend at odd angles. A few feet away, a red-haired woman is calmly gutting and deboning a rabbit, its eyes glassy and final. It is a scene of perfect self-sufficiency and care. Nell wonders if it has been choreographed for her. And yet the contrast between the practicality of the act and the woman's bloodied hands unnerves her. The woman in the wheelchair stares at her, momentarily in fear, until a blankness descends. Nell follows Sile back towards the building.

13

The room allocated for the studio is junk-filled and unre-markable. Maman had asked one of the novices to move some boxes, and Nell tries to clear a path. An easel is propped against the back wall. There are stacks of old plates and cups. A Singer sewing machine with a wrought-iron pedal, an ancient piano, communion chalices and several laundry hampers. In one corner, a storage heater with a frayed plug stands mournfully. The air smells of dust and stored vegetables. She will tidy today, put some order to the chaos and begin work tomorrow.

By the time the room is in reasonable shape, it is dark. An ache has started low in her spine and there is a cut on her left hand. She takes in the room again. Another lamp wouldn't hurt. Old buildings reveal their stories at night. It will take time to gauge the energy of the place. She expects to hear footsteps or movement, but there is only silence. Nell feels a dampness in the air settle on her skin and a brief wariness. The sense of something changing irrefuta-bly. As she moves a stack of old books, she thinks of the bible she'd sent the Iníons. The making of the project is a haze. Made during a bleak time when she was taking pills to stay awake, then throwing back whiskey to sleep. It's a miracle she got through it. The piece was called *Et Super Matres Dolorem: et Feminam Vulgate*, 'The Mothers of Sorrow: A Female Bible'. With four new gospels by women to replace Matthew, Mark, Luke, and John. The ink bled through the first mock-up, but she loved the feel of that thin bible paper. One of the gospels she attributed to Danu, offering a vision of a new world where people worshipped the land and not a god. All four new gospels were rooted in some way in old creation stories. That a woman created the world, one reinvented the Kurgan hypothesis, the idea of Mitochondrial Eve. The whole thing was meant to be both political and a wry provocation. That anyone still read ancient, autocratic texts and lived their lives by them was ridiculous. Nell wanted to satirise that, but also offer new stories. Imagining the world if women had run things for centuries, or if our figures of worship were not so often men. Or maybe not even human. If the sea ruled the world, or the trees. These ideas permeate all of her work.

The Gideons would have been horrified. The parish bishop denounced the book with accusations of blasphemy. Radio call-in shows were plagued. A local politician (who lived on the mainland, and never came to the island) called her a heathen. And yet this isolated group up on the cliffs had embraced it. It is so clear now, why they've asked her. She was beginning to understand their withdrawal, living so far from the rest of the world. A small queendom.

Later, Ebele arrives with a storage heater. It fills the air with a nauseous kind of heat. Nell thanks her and picks up a handful of folders and spreads them on the desk. They contain what appear to be detailed accounts of the lives of the women. A few have included their old names, the ones they used before they came here. Some sections have been blacked out. Many have had terrible experiences – violence, poverty, grief. Lives scuttled like ships. As she sifts through the pages, the weight of their stories presses down on Nell. Terrible stories always made her resolve to do more with her time. Make more art. Better choices. Mortality is a specific kind of motivator. Nell's life has differed so much from theirs, but they are not so dissimilar. United in wanting to feel that they've contributed something to the world. The book will be a marker that they existed, that they've been here.

14

The Iníons arrived three decades ago, but other people have been here for longer than the living can remember. Some stay simply because generations of their family did. The island has a way of tethering people to the soil, despite high watermarks of loss. Even when people leave, stories survive. One more than others. A century ago, a pernicious strain of blight caused all the root crops to fail. People fought over supplies and the island starved. Women were the greatest casualties; those breastfeeding were sucked dry. Malnutrition contributed to plummeting conception rates. Then, that Easter, a group of young wives went missing from their homes.

A storm blew all week, the sky a mackerel shade. Local men – desperate, hungry – gathered to look for them. On the third day, near Danu's cliff, they heard moaning and took it for a trapped animal. Something that could be killed and eaten. Moving towards the noise, they saw the missing women gathered on the ground, frantically scratching, their nails small brown crescents of dirt. Scoop-shoving the damp earth with a steady rhythm. When the men questioned them, the women didn't slow or raise their eyes.

We're looking for children.

As though there were infant tubers under the soil.

You have to dig longer for boys.

Late in that wretched year – everyone bone-hollow, stomachs shrunk – the sound came again. As if the year had not been ominous enough with its rumble of notes. In its wake came a seismic wave that grabbed at coastal cottages, pulling thin bodies back to the sea. They resembled wretched flotsam, sticks in the water. Each body is a reservoir. Of bloodied waters. Of the things that can destroy us.

Since those days there are no longer any big families on the island. The year-round population has never quite recovered. Each summer, numbers swell, and the accompanying seasonal glut suits most people. The islanders are grateful for crowds and their money. The change of pace. In winter, everything contracts again. In those hard months, you never see a soul out on the roads after 4.30 p.m., and the grey-green waters become more treacherous.

Nell tried to make an installation about those haunted, digging women. The project got under her skin. Each night she'd wake up, convinced they were gathered around her bed, pulling at the sheets. She'd run to wash the soil from under her nails. Some of the women at Rathglas were mothers. More than one of the testimonies talked about leaving children behind.

15

In the dark, Cleary waits. The air up at the forest is dank, leaden. In the distance, the town has few streetlights, but the landing strip of the main street is visible. Out beyond that, the lighthouse is engaged in its sentry sweep.

The undergrowth stirs. He should have changed the torch batteries. Uncle Jimmy brings two or three extra pairs. Disgustingly organised. Not like Cleary's father. All those nights they climbed Screen's Hill as darkness mantled the town. His old man sea-gnarled and weary. At the first fingers of dawn light, he'd sling the catch over his shoulder, nodding to indicate they were done. On the way down, his whistling sounded louder in the half-light.

Near the end, Cleary Senior told stories about the Somme. Unlike many islanders, he hadn't spent his life wishing he'd left. He'd never even been to the mainland, never mind France. *Corporal! Private! Lieutenant!* Cannons and mustard gas. Grim tales of waking up in inches of water. A mattress of mud and piss. Misty-eyed laments for a sweetheart back home. His wife of thirty-seven years patiently spooning mushy egg-in-a-cup into his lax mouth. Some days at the chime of the Angelus bell, he'd leap out of bed and sing with spitty, shouty fervour.

Hagstone

Where the land is low
Like a huge imprisoning O
I hear a heart that's sound and high.
I hear the heart within me cry:
I'm homesick for my hills again

The heartsick notes of it. The feel of the plastic hospital chair under Cleary's arse, not the soft bed of soil. He pushes the memory aside. Readjusts his whole self: arms, shoulders, face. Waiting, ready. It feels good to reacquaint himself with the wind up here.

A crackle. He listens; his whole mind focused on his ear, blood surging there from every direction. Breath and concentration. Not light-footed enough for a fox, too heavy to be a rabbit. Hand ready on the lamp, thumb twitching over the switch. A shadow. Something ducks, hides, considers for a minute. Cleary shrinks into himself, concealed by ferns and the low branches of a pine.

– Jimmy, you fucker! You scared the life out of me. Jesus.

A hiss of laughter, gas escaping from a pipe, before his uncle's face moves into view. He'd know that silhouette anywhere, with its sloping shoulders. Once a redhead, he's greyer now, his beard salt and paprika.

– Thought you said you weren't coming …

– Nothing doing in the town tonight – what the fuck else was I going to do?

Jimmy is perpetually unemotional. Whether he was proposing to someone, or signing a contract, his face would bear the same expression. Even after the docs told him about the tumour in his lung.

– What'd you bring?

– Gel filters. Orange ones. More batteries. Wouldn't trust you, ye fool.

– Orange?

– Softer. Better than the red. For night vision.

He pulls cigarette papers from a pocket, adding a pinch of tobacco.

– Don't light up, for fuck's sake. You'll give us away.

– How's the cottage suiting you?

– It's grand, thanks. Really appreciate it.

– No bother, son.

Jimmy has always called him that, even though he's only ten years older. He has no children of his own. Never married but has lived a hectic life. Every island has a Jimmy Cleary. The guy who always got in on the ground business-wise. Built the mini-mart, sold diesel. Even owned Ryan's for years but drank more than he sold. A decade sober now. With his Big Man persona, it was inevitable he'd try politics. First as island mayor, and later representing the mainland constituency the island was part of. But it was an unremarkable career. No committee roles, let alone a ministerial position. He bided his time on the back benches, grateful for the pension. In a snap election, he eventually lost his seat.

– How's life?

– Ack.

– Work?

– Same, but busy – you free on Thursday? Ollie Downes
has a lame horse needs sorting.

His uncle has scaled life down completely. Owns a small
incinerator and runs a business disposing of fallen stock.
Farmers bring him their dead: lame horses, cast ewes, cattle
with broken legs. He doesn't really need to work. He made
his money long ago.

– Sure. Pick me up at two, yeah?

Jimmy nods, swills a sour glob of spit around and sends
it into the air.

– Still seeing that English woman, boss?

– Nope. Too much hassle. There's a gorgeous Latvian
working up in the B&B. Thought she'd head home after the
summer but she's still here. Christ, have you seen her?

Everyone had. She's not Cleary's type. Too thin, too
frosty, blonde.

– Yeah, nice-looking girl.

A sudden image of the woman on the beach. Dark waves
of wet hair, plastered to her face. Jimmy would know who
she was but asking would make him vulnerable. It's risky
too. His uncle is a bigmouth. Their manner with each other
is of men who prefer practical things to talking.

– Keeping busy?

Jimmy isn't the tender sort but checks in on him.

– Same ol', same ol'.

– You settling back in OK?

– Yeah. I've a bit of work coming up on the boats.

The waves in the bay below turn over, but it's too high to hear the sound.

– What about you?

Cleary gestures to the older man's chest.

– Grand. I take the tablets. They make me go to the mainland for a scan every three months. Could be worse.

They are quiet, mutually keen to change the subject. Cleary glances at his uncle. Jimmy could be thinking about his failing chest. Or erotic thoughts about the B&B girl. He might be thinking about how long he has left and whether he has made good choices or bad. If he should have travelled more. Married. Been kinder.

The wind moves up the hill, picking its way over rocks. Movement. Slight, but coordinated. Jimmy raises the lamp discreetly to show he hears it too. They wait. A shadow darts from a mound of undergrowth. Cleary taps twice on Jimmy's shoulder to get ready.

Finally, after what feels like hours, the last light streaks out of the sky. Another hour and the darkness will be absolute. They can make out the shadow moving in small skittering circles, stopping to sniff. There could be more than one, but they cannot tell at night. He's hefty though. A male, Cleary reckons. The creature stops, still, head cocked. Does it hear them?

Cleary raises his shotgun, digs the stock into his clavicle. Gives a single tap on Jimmy's shoulder and curls his finger round the trigger. The lamp snaps on, its focus tight, and the glade is pooled in pale orange light. It's a hare, not a rabbit. Imposing, it stares back. The hare is frozen, blinded by the lamp, the searing peach shade. Cleary has done this countless times, feeling a mixture of thrill and guilt. Bagging rabbits, never a fox. Not worth killing something you can't cook. It's rare to find a hare this far up the hill. Most days at sunset they're down near the sea. His mother used to see them in the garden when she was working in the kitchen. Churning suds in a basin for the dishes, out of the corner of her eye there'd be a flash of brown; two muscular legs bounding past shrubs and out onto the ragged shingle of the shore.

Jimmy hisses, meaning that it will be too late if he doesn't shoot. Cleary aims, squeezes and hears the sound bounce off the trees. A ringing in his ears.

– Nice one, son.

Jimmy pats him on the back.

– A fucking beast of thing. Grand bit of meat on it too.

– Pint? For you, I mean.

– Many pints.

Cleary thinks now that he should have said something to the woman on the beach. Not just walked off. Asked her name even. Darkness has crowded in fast. In the pool of Jimmy's lamp they stand, loosening their aching muscles. The hills up here hold on to things. Gunshot vapour, pellets of rabbit shit, drunken fumbles imprinted on every blade of grass.

16

At night Nell cruises the roads, taking the hairpin corners at speed for the heck of it. Listening to music, drowning out the high winds. The car, in an act of divination, knows where to go. She parks in the shadows of the lane below, walking up the furrowed track to his cottage. There are no lights on, no stove smoke.

Disappointment and irritation coagulate.

Back at the car, she revs the engine and turns the music up. Tries to light a cigarette, but the charger cable is where the lighter should be. She gropes in the well between the seats, or under the blowers that only work on the lowest speed. Slamming the heels of her hand on the wheel, she speeds up, wondering if there are matches in the glove compartment. Curse that fucking lighter. This stupid car.

She's not far from the town when she sees him.

Stumbling with the asymmetric gusto of a man who's been drinking for hours. There's no path on this stretch of road, and the car almost grazes his arm as he sways into the gorse. She drives on, pulling in at a farm gate round the bend. Sits, engine off, eyes on the rear-view mirror. The fear another car might hit him before he appears.

Should she have sounded the horn on the way past? An acknowledgement. Perhaps it will seem odd now, her sitting at the roadside in the dark. She restarts the car quickly and an old song comes on. One that would have caused tears at any other time. She spins the dial to silent. How long did they speak for on the beach that day – a minute? Two? He may not remember her face at all.

This is merely the act of a good Samaritan.

You tell yourself that.

An immediate, erotic image of his hands on her. Clothes tugged. All mouths.

STOP IT.

He finally shows up in the mirror, clocking the car for the first time. Nell leans over and rolls down the passenger window.

– Hey there – you look like a man in need of a lift?

A casual shrug while leaning on the door. The waft of an evening's worth of pints. The indicator ticks, a tiny metronome soundtracking the scene. He turns away to face the road, as if gauging the distance, or the darkness, or the stupidity of walking the rest of the way so late.

– Suppose so, yeah, thanks. Up ahead there.

He tumbles in, laughing in a way he had seemed incapable of the day on the beach. Goofy almost, childlike. A vague wrist flick to indicate direction and they move off into the night. He's hammered and she envies it. Wishing they both were in the same state. That the hours before this had been them huddled together, chatting over pints. Telling the stories everyone tells at the start of things. She makes an exaggerated show of adjusting the mirror, wishing there weren't crisp packets and bits of driftwood on the floor. Cleary, beer-fuelled and fuzzy, is oblivious to the grime. The crumbs gathered in the rubber cuff of the gear stick.

– Nice motor.

– This old yoke?

– Yeah. Not fancy. Clean.

– Ha! That heap of pints is affecting your eyes. It's actually manky.

She laughs. He says nothing and fiddles with the radio. Rotates the tuning left and right. A glitchy longwave frequency wails in the speakers.

– Jesus … Leave it!

Another giddy laugh. She wants to ask about his night. Who he was with. Instead, she focuses on the road.

– Just lookin' for tunes, is all.

She reaches into the well beside the handbrake and hands him a CD folder. Plastic pockets, titles scrawled in black marker.

– The signal is crap around here, so this is my analogue backup.

After a struggle with the zip, he flips through, theatrically slapping the plastic. *Oh god.* Nell hasn't listened to any of it in ages. A lot of drone rock. Bulgarian folk music. A lame euro dance compilation for running. He eases a disc into the slot. Deep breath.

– Now this … this is a fucking tune.

The plaintive piano of Bowie's 'Life on Mars' begins and there's a distinct possibility that she might die. Pass away right there at the wheel of the car and kill them both. The lyrics of her teenage years. The song she listened to after the first time her heart was trodden on. But now, if something ever happens between them – big and wild and intense – and it doesn't work out, this song will be added to the pathetic soundtrack of her adult life. Extending the credits, weeping in the dark of the cinema.

She half expects him to sing along, swaying with the sailors fighting in the dance hall, but he is quiet. The childish laugh drained away. A sudden fear that he might get sick all over the car.

– You feeling OK?

A quick calculation. No driveways on this stretch. If all else fails, there's a large crisp bag by his feet. Snacks for that nocturnal routine outside his cottage. Fidgety, he shifts in the seat and turns to face her, antiseptic breath filling the air. More than anything she wants to look back at him. Up this close.

– So why haven't we ever met? In person like …

– Dunno. Have you been off island?

She plays dumb, slows the car to make the journey last longer.

– Yeah. A few years. I'm only just home.

– How you finding being back?

A stupid question. Obvious. He doesn't answer.

– Appreciate the lift. I'm not far from here.

– Just say when to turn.

– Near the edge of the forest.

– I'm very fond of these woods. I walk here a lot.

– Ah, wait! Yes, *now* I know you.

Panic rushes up, a tide spreading over legs, stomach, chest. The smile is unnerving. He knows. She imagines slamming the car into a tree.

– You're the sand girl …

– The *what?*

It's possible Cleary is more drunk than he appears.

– That day on the beach … you said you were checking out the sand.

The project. Oh god. The relief.

– Ah yes … and you told me off for swimming.

Deliberately casual. Pretending the penny has just dropped.

– You were mermaiding about the place – which might seem grand to you – but you could get yourself killed swimming there. It's happened before.

Her hands are welded to the wheel, guiding them around blind bends. She could drive these roads with someone's hands over her eyes. His maybe, the ridges of his thumbs. Head line, heart line, life line …

– I always thought it was a cruel trick that, for an island, there's only so many decent places to swim. Let the tourists have the beach by the harbour. I get sick of the same thing, the same places. The curse of living here, I suppose …

She trails off as the road dips. Cleary leans nearer, seat belt straining, eyes slightly glazed.

– Hold on. It's not just from the beach …

Now, an immense gratitude to be legally obligated to keep her eyes on the road. He might have seen her the other night. The gears grind, necessitating an ostentatious manoeuvre of the stick, making a drama of switching from third to second. And then, portentous and welcome, the tall pine at the entrance to the cottage lane appears, offered like a biblical miracle. The car bounces on the hardened muck. Morning will be here in a matter of hours, forcepped out of the night. Outside the cottage, she stops the car. He is serious now, the booze moving off him.

– You *do* know where I live …

– I know the forest. It's a small island, we all know everywhere.

– That's not what I'm talking about.

She is done for. He will tell everyone. The talk about the bungalow couple will resurface. It will be a reason to leave for good. In a crisis, Nell is a quick thinker – all liars are – but she has nothing in this moment, no way to talk her way out of it.

– If you don't know where I live, then why do you stand outside my window?

The car fills with dread. When she turns to him, a shock. There is no indignation or disgust. Instead, on his face – a small, coy smile teetering.

Before Nell can offer any feeble explanation, he lurches forward, grabbing the phone from the dashboard cradle. Bowie is still murmuring low like a priest. Cleary concentrates in an almost comical manner, tapping at the screen. He replaces it and dials. A rectangle lights up in his shirt pocket.

– There. You have me, and I have you.

Nell is silent. Massively impressed that he didn't embarrass her, and by this act of initiative.

– OK then.

– Get back to me on why you hang around outside my gaff. Or you know, if you want to go for a drink?

He exits with more agility and speed than he fell in with. Before she can say anything, he palm-slaps the roof of the car goodbye.

She watches him in the mirror, struggling with the key in the lock.

You have me, and I have you.

Down the road, Nell brakes heavily and picks the phone off the seat. There, in sleek characters:

CLEARY

17

The studio at Rathglas looks out on to what resembles a neat garden, the sea in the distance. Surrounded by low hedging, cut off from the bustle of chickens and sheds. Benches overlook a small pond, painstakingly made by Ebele. Some Iníons gather there for yoga or group meditation in the mornings. Today, a few are assembled on the benches, talking quietly. Nell could have prised the window a sliver wide to listen in, but it felt wrong. The testimonies were one version of their lives. But, to tell their story, she will have to get to know these women. She closes the door and heads for the garden.

Voices lower as she appears, standing apart from them until one Iníon raises a hand and beckons her over. The young pale girl from the first day.

– Hello again, it's Sile, right?

She is small, with an open, relaxed face, and nods at Nell. Everything about her suggests someone used to looking after people.

– Hi – only if you're sure you don't mind? I feel like I'm butting in.

– Not at all – this is Ebele, Rose, Z, Aurora, Aisling, Sadhbh and Muireann. And myself, of course.

The women glance at Nell, a mix of curiosity and hesitance. All except Sadhbh, who is shelling peas into a bowl and does not look up.

– Hello to you all – I can sit over there if I'm intruding. I just came out for a bit of air.

Ebele urges them to make room on the bench. Nell sits. Aisling is eating an apple the way a dog might chew a bone, masticating with a rhythm that distorts her face. Z is combing knots from the hair of Aurora, who sits at her feet. Sile looks at her shyly, and from one face to another, hoping someone will include Nell, or at least not be rude. There is a sense they have not been consulted about her visit.

– Are you from the island?

Nell nods. This is Z.

– Yes, just up that big bendy road. The state of it – my arse is black and blue from the bike saddle.

A couple of the Iníons snort.

– I remember that road. Someone from the town gave me a lift after I handed over my last twenty quid. She wrote her phone number on my hand because she was sure I'd be straight back out.

Nell isn't sure if Aisling or Aurora is speaking. The whirl of names went by too fast for her and it seems impolite to ask again. Aurora perhaps? Eyes the colour of rock pools.

– At least you were given a phone number. No one spoke to me at all when I got off the boat. Had to make my own way here alone.

– And don't get me started on that overnight ferry. Jesus, I prayed like I never prayed before on that crossing.

The group laugh, relaxing a little. They range in age from twenties to fifties. Nothing gives away each individual's roles or skills, their quirks or habits. Except Sadhbh, repetitively popping peas. From a small fabric loop on her smock hangs a large bunch of keys, which suggests authority, or position. Nell is aware how important it is to ease in, to appear friendly but not nosy.

– How long have you all been here?

The group falls quiet. Aisling and Rose exchange a look.

– Nine years. Best decision I ever made.

This is Ebele, who brought her the heater. There is a warm, matter-of-factness to her. Nell liked her immediately.

– I bet you never get tired of this v—

Rose, her mouth flat and sharp as a blade, stands up abruptly and heads for the main building. The group quieten, and Nell senses they are embarrassed. It was probably a mistake to have joined them today. Maman is nowhere to be seen.

– Well, I'll leave you all to it. I'm holed up in that little room near the stairs … the door is always open.

– Thank you, Nell. We wish you well with the project, *Suaimhneas*.

She moves across the grass, slightly mortified. *Stickleback, stickleback, run away home.* A scrap of song she made up as a kid in honour of this feeling of being excluded. Or when she'd stay too late playing in the forest and fear settled on her. Glancing back, the women are huddled together, listening to Rose, who has now sloped back to them, and seems to be issuing instructions. *Stickleback, Stickleback, show me the moon.*

18

It was impossible to exactly predict the arrival of the sound. The cannonball rumble of it. It paid no heed to scientific forecasts. Storm warnings in traffic light colours. Some felt it in advance, like a tingle on the skin. Others said the air felt heavier. Last night, it arrived along with a new moon. The result was something never seen before. The women of the island woke in their beds to a familiar, unwelcome sensation. Some feared their bladders had given way, until they rolled back the covers. Every single one had bled a river, a crimson Rorschach test on the sheets. It did not discriminate against age or fertility: pre-pubescent girls were among those reporting mass haemorrhaging. Even Veronica Doyle, the oldest woman on the island, coming up on ninety-five. Nell too woke to blood on her sheets. A tiny reservoir of rust. Her own blood, despite its familiarity, sometimes brought up thoughts of war. The Somme. Poppies. Chests punctured by bayonets in swift lines.

Strangest of all, the women who were pregnant bled, and in fevered panic, shook the sleeping limbs of their husbands awake, fearing the worst. But the babies were intact, nestled into the curve of their mother's spine.

The Iníons, despite their seclusion, were not immune. The women scrubbing clots like raisins off sheets and underwear, from the backs of smocks. Out in the cliff garden at Rathglas that morning, rows of bedsheets billowed on the clothes line like open sails. The sound gone for now, the island returned to itself again.

19

The day after the sound came, Nell works at home, making notes and sketches. By evening, she is starving and boils water in a large pot to make soup, lining up spices, grating garlic. She nicks a finger but ignores it when a song she loves comes on the radio, sung by a famous soprano. It always makes her think of watching someone you've desired for a long time approach you with the same look of pure longing. The moment of knowing that you were going to get exactly what you want. Like that first wave when the forest mushrooms hit. Lust as psilocybin. The notes climb and Nell sings as high as her voice will allow, falling far short of the soprano's level.

On the opposite counter is a bucket containing the skull of a stoat. Nell has stripped and cleaned it close to the bone, but to remove the remaining flesh, it is steeped in hydrogen peroxide, a kind of maceration. Her task tonight is to reattach the mandible and any teeth that have come loose. It could work as part of a future project. A familiar problem. Starting too many things, ideas like dodgems, colliding in her head. The shed out by the veg patch is crammed with half-made pieces and things she plans to use. Five shop mannequins, one without a head; ostrich feathers dyed in coral pink, a jar of her own blood. Anyone wandering in there by mistake would think it a macabre bricolage. The bones of a life's work. Every part of it personal, imbued with some meaning yet to reveal itself, even to Nell. There might be something there that she can use for the Iníons' commission. These thoughts run parallel to ones of Cleary.

The song comes to an end, and she scrapes carrots and parsnips into the boiling pot. It has been raining heavily, vapour streaks the windows and fills the kitchen with steam. These are the nights when she feels most content. That there is no point to leaving, or long complicated journeys of exile. What can the world offer her that she doesn't already have? Everything she needs is here.

On the counter, her phone buzzes, shifting to the right. She rinses the last of the veg peel from her hands and picks it up.

I'm outside.

A charge moves through her. A bold move. Skin dotted with sweat; she wishes there'd been time to shower. Discarding the apron, she moves towards the front door and unlocks it. He is leaning on the jamb – angular, suggestive – a move she will later learn is a quirk of his. A distinct means of introduction, that makes him appear both aloof and curious.

The look of him. That clean sweep of jaw, his slight stoop. The mark on his face, glistening. And the way he is looking at her. He steps in, his shoulders speckled with rain, hair damp and in disarray.

– Give me a sec – need to turn down the cooker.

This buys a few seconds to think. About what has made him walk all the way up here on such a bad night. Perhaps he isn't here for why she wants him to be. *I need to borrow a shovel. There's been a death on the island. Thanks for getting my pissed arse home safely.*

She hopes it is none of these things.

Any minute now, he will say, 'I'm not staying', a phrase that makes her lonely before the other person has even gone. When she returns to the small front room, he is exactly where she left him. Coat dripping in an impressive boundary around him. They are several feet apart and she wants to say something. Any word. A joke, maybe. To push something into the space between them.

When it happens, it is abrupt, without formality. He strides towards her, and his mouth is on hers, gripping the back of her neck, pulling her in. He tastes of mint, and she is oddly touched by the preparation. Wrenching the wet mass of coat from his shoulders, while he pulls at the buttons on her top, pressing her onto the couch. Hands move over skin. The ice of them makes her flinch. The weight of him, his arched back, the hips she has coveted through the mould-flecked cottage window. His movements are deft. There are words she can't make out, an instruction folded into her ear as though it were a note.

Blood pounds in her ears.

This is it.

20

The Iníons are a tight group, despite their schisms. It's possible that some came to Rathglas because they feared spending their life alone. It's not something she senses from Maman, who seems to thrive on the solitude, bustling around when needed. Occasionally, she enquires on progress, but Nell is mostly left alone to work. The others keep a respectful distance, with one exception. Muireann seeks her out. Shy at first, she brings tea to the studio, offers to show Nell around their patch of cliff.

Most days she is at Rathglas, Nell sees Muireann make for the cove below the cliff in search of what the waves have thrown up. The ladder down is measled with rust. Salt has eroded the paint, but the structure is solid. On the shore, she gathers anything that could be recycled or reused. Afterwards, she has taken to dropping by the studio with bits and pieces that might be of use for Nell's art. Sea glass, dead starfish, unusual rocks or shells. The Iníons have been instructed by Maman to give Nell space and avoid asking about her personal life or the world beyond the gate. But Muireann is talkative. Wants to know about family, relationships, her art. The other women's stories are familiar, or at least the ones they feel comfortable sharing. Muireann promised to show her the cove and stops by the studio first with a small object rolled up in a piece of fabric, which she hands over.

Nell unwraps it, touched at the gesture.

– A hagstone – I have a thing for them! Thank you.

– For years I just thought they were battered stones with holes in them, until Sile set me right. About the fact they're lucky, and fishermen tie them to their boats to ward off evil.

– And that if you look through the hole, you're meant to see a different view of the world. I think that's why I collect them. Looking, seeing, an artist thing.

– Come down and see the cove with me. We can find some more of these.

They move down the ladder onto the stones, and Muireann hands over a bucket to pick through. Old limpet shells, razor clam shells, the kind of blue it almost hurts to look at.

– You've never actually told me about your art – what kind of stuff is it?

– Oh fuck, I don't know. No one likes explaining their work.

– Tell me!

Muireann laughs, lobbing a tiny shell at her.

– I think I'm trying to make something about infinity. Or symbols of infinity. Ever heard of the ouroboros? You know, the snake eating its own head? Or the lemniscate – the thing that looks like a number eight on its side. I keep coming back to circles. The whole infinite line thing. I'm sort of obsessed. There's a French artist – Louise Bourgeois – and she made spirals. My plan, a sort of homage, is to make the biggest one I can, on Banshla.

Muireann listens, absently stacking a pile of small shells.

– You know I shouldn't be talking to you about this?

– Why?

– Maman warned me about talking about the outside world to you all, so—

– Oh, she says a lot of things. A new face, new stories, is a breath of fresh air.

Nell pushes another pile of similar-sized shells towards Muireann.

– Well then, if you don't mind, can I ask why you came here?

Muireann straightens up, considering the question. Nell wonders if the women confide in each other about their old lives. About the alliances. Who gets on, who avoids who.

– It's been five years since last May. I was an addict. Total mess. The fact of it is, the world just didn't suit me. I wanted oblivion, not the same old same old. Couldn't hold down a job. Struggled for rent, mooched around. I'm better in a group. And sober.

– That's really tough.

– Ah it's grand, much more myself these days. It's fine. I just got sick of every day feeling like the end of the world.

– I think we all feel like that sometimes.

– Do you?

– Not in a major way. I couldn't ever say that I suffer the way some do. But … I have my bad days like anyone else. I think that's why I tend to keep to myself too. It's just less hassle.

– But do you get lonely, living on your own, on a small island?

– God no, I love it. That said, I'm really enjoying the company here. Well, you, anyway. I'm still waiting for most of the others to get used to me.

They watch a couple of gannets diving for fish.

– Does this place help you, living with all these other people?

– I think so. But moving away … you still have to lug all your brain shit with you. I still feel like I could have been better. That I *should* have been more. Maybe if I *had* been more, I wouldn't have gone off on constant benders and let people down. But that's on me. And it's a day-to-day thing. I used to think of my life as a ruin. One of those old collapsed churches or a castle, shedding bricks each year, the arch of each window struggling to stay upright. But I'm trying to do the conservation. Working through the shame.

Nell thinks about this. The shame of not being more successful. The opportunities she turned down because it would have meant leaving the island.

– Shame can be useful, though. For keeping people in their place.

– How do you mean?

Muireann holds her gaze, as if about to say something but decides against it.

– It can be a tool. And no matter where you go, college or the local Neighbourhood Watch, someone always wants to have the run of things, don't they?

– Absolute power corrupts absolutely.

– Something like that.

– Anyway ... I don't rate shame. Shame can fuck right off.

Muireann laughs. Nell notices a tiny birthmark on her cheek that bends into a crescent. A minuscule moon on her face.

21

Maman takes the ledger from her drawer, sifting through the pages. Making notes and calculations. Anxious that the range in the kitchen is on its last legs. The old pipes are gurgling with sludge. It's hard to keep everything going. Bearing responsibility for so many things. But this is her calling. The work she was destined to do. The weight of it wakes her in the night, on the ones she manages to sleep, instead of sitting at the window following the moon. It would help to go to the kitchen, warm some milk, but the building feels different to her at night. The gloomy corridors and pitch-black corners. Resigned, she sits and waits for the dawn instead. These are the nights she thinks of the old city she lived in. Of the protests. Her old job. On wakeful nights she traces a path from that life to this one, year by year. Each mistake, every loss, right up to the early days at Rathglas. There were some real firebrands back then. But kind too. They looked out for the younger ones. The energy was different. Heightened, competitive. Like the power struggle at the start of a relationship.

She wonders what Nell makes of the testimonies. The Iníons shedding the world like a skin. It's possible that

whatever they abandoned at the gate is still out there waiting, growing more malignant. What is Nell's story? Maman
wonders why she said yes. They couldn't offer much in the
way of a fee and the work is basic enough. But then every-
body is motivated by something. Greed, lust, pain. Or
maybe material – Nell will probably make work about her
time here. There is nothing to be done about that. They
have not yet bonded in the way Maman hoped they would,
but Nell has been respectful of the other Iníons. The chats
with the group in the garden made her uneasy. She had
gravitated towards Muireann. Of course she had. As long as
she knew her place, and finished the book, all would be
well.

22

The early days of a new thing are unequalled in any part of
life. Nell and Cleary are ravenous. For food, booze, each
other. Nell constantly feels that she wants to bite into his
flesh to affirm his realness, or keep him near – a coin in a
pocket, a scarf wrapped tight. Away from Rathglas, on her
tour this week, mid-spiel about the shipwreck in the bay,
she is thinking about all the things they could do to each
other.

They have fucked in the woods; rattled the walls of
corrugated barns, his mould-speckled cottage, her warm
front room. Once, in a small trawler they stole. While he
worked his way into her flesh from behind, she turned her
head away from the discarded bucket of fish bits, cleavered
like Manx tails. The torn pages of a calendar.

She is becoming familiar with every inch of his cottage.
One afternoon in bed she kept her eyes fixed on the window
throughout. The one that she had once been outside of,
separate from, and unknown to him. The reversal has made
her wonder if she'd had far more power out there, after all.
An old feeling returning, even as he sighs and groans
beneath her.

Some nights she sits in the tub just to soothe her body from the fact that they could not stop themselves. The rawness below, the bruises that bloom days later. Nell senses he's all in, after just a week, but she isn't sure of this yet. She wants only uncomplicatedness. Clean lines. Monochrome. For now, all she craves is bliss.

23

Cleary stayed again last night and when she woke, he was already gone. The sheets creased, the bed chill. In the shower, she scoops a dead moth out of the drain. Ten minutes later, she's cycling up the lane, rain coating her face, delicious on her tongue. Her bones feel lighter, something turns over – a wheel down a hill – thinking of her life. The goodness of it. It's so unexpected that this kind of desire would come her way. But it's a distraction too. Another thing demanding her time.

The morning's work at Rathglas involves sifting through old maps of the grounds. Considerable effort has been made to preserve and build around the chapel, which predates St Brigid's by centuries. Nell wonders who decided to build it on such a remote part of the island. She could sketch it for the book, include illustrations of the grounds alongside the testimonies.

From the window, she can see some Iníons eating lunch on the benches. She tracks cloud shapes: a running stoat, a big-chinned witch, a shark with one fin. All gathered like the baleen frill of a whale's mouth.

Lenticular.

Cumulus.

Mammatus.

(Literally, tit cloud.)

She laughs.

Her breasts used to be better. Her whole body is changing. Whenever the despondency this inspires gets too much,
she trawls a website for death announcements. Pages of
elderly people who die old and content in hospices.
Tragically, Suddenly, After a long illness bravely borne.
Death lingo. A read-between-the-lines knack to spot the
tragic suicides. Murder cases with hundreds of condolence
messages from strangers. *A concerned mother. A local man.*
Mostly she clicks on photos of people who look her age. A
memento mori.

She needs to stop anthropomorphising clouds. And the
rest. She is convinced that her garden has a soul. That the
lighthouse is an old man. The sea, a restless woman.

The group in the garden are starting to thin out. If she's
quick, she'll catch them. The testimonies are historical and
Nell suspects some of them might feel far removed from the
person who first walked through the gates. How many of
them have changed? Has this place provided whatever it
was they arrived looking for? Most people navigate life by
the same kind of rituals: day and night, meals and jobs.
Love, if they're lucky. An unwavering template. Those who
seek anything outside that are cursed.

Moving across the grass, Nell hears singing coming from
somewhere in the building. Choral, distant, the rise and fall

of vaguely religious notes. And from behind the hedge, the low hiss of an argument. When she arrives, the women are startled but welcoming.

– Good morning, Nell.

The subject has clearly been changed. Muireann shunts up on the bench and pats a place beside her. Rose stares pointedly out to sea.

– How are you all this morning?

Ebele and Z are quiet. Rose smirks and Nell can't quite figure out what's going on.

– We were talking about the ghost.

The others look at the ground. Sile looks uncomfortable.

– A ghost?

– Yes, has no one told you?

– I've never heard there was a ghost here.

– Well, you've never been out here before. Did you not do any research before you came?

Rose is warming up, ready to spar, picking at the flaking skin pooled on one elbow. Just as Nell is about to reply, Maman appears out of nowhere.

– Good morning, Iníons. Nell, I'm glad to see you're meeting the sisters.

A fleck of shiny, dried egg clings to the front of her smock. Rose and Sile excuse themselves.

– Nell, I was looking for you, actually – could you drop by my office if you have a moment? Only if you're free.

Nell nods, unsure of what just happened. She should get back to the studio. The ghost might have been the subject of the conversation, but she suspects a wind-up. At home, she wouldn't have to deal with whatever this game was. About now, the sun would be moving across the sitting room, making shadows of the fireplace scuttle, throwing gold shapes on the rug. She would lie down, tucked round the heat of it and ignore Rose's animosity. A small rectangle of sun always made her feel safe.

She waits a polite amount of time and makes her way to the office. Off the corridor outside the room, on the back stairs, Aurora is quietly weeping. Still unsure of her place, Nell hesitates about intruding on this moment of private despair. Muireann has hinted at tension in the house but assured her it was nothing to do with her presence. Sadhbh and Rose have not warmed to her, and she feared it would spread through the group, a kind of contagion, but most of the women have offered only kindness. She moves towards Aurora and places a hand on her shoulder. On the upper floor, someone is singing a plaintive song in the old language. They listen without speaking and Aurora pats Nell's hand, gathers herself and continues up the staircase.

There is no way of knowing if any of the women came here only to feel stuck but have committed to it as a permanent home. Getting what you want is not always what you need, in the end. Nell craves privacy, aligning herself with a very different kind of solitude to that of the Iníons. She has been too long alone, adrift even, in so many aspects of life that it is impossible to consider another way.

When she arrives, the door is open and Maman is standing by the impressive window, back turned. Nell has often seen her in this stance from outside, surveying the women working below. In the distance, a small group are building a perimeter fence for the root vegetable patch. Nell raps a knuckle softly on the door, and Maman turns, her face tensed by whatever deep thought preoccupied her before being disturbed.

– Ah, Nell. Good. Sit.

She fusses around, a little matronly, quick on her feet.

– I see you're settling in and getting to know everyone?

Nell nods but does not disclose what just happened.

– Very good. You'll find that not everyone here is running from something. Each finds their own way to live. Muireann among the plants. Sile glad of a gang of surrogate sisters – she's an only child, you know.

It isn't clear why she is being told this, but she listens, taking it all in.

There is a quick, strained look.

– You know, it's probably best that you – perhaps – keep a bit of distance?

– From the other women? I'm mostly in the studio on my own, but I get out for air sometimes and can't avoid running into people.

– Oh, I get that, of course, but just … maybe you don't want to get too involved … you know, just for the book, objectivity and all that. 'Authorial distance' – is that what they call it?

Nell is unsure if this is a warning, but she knows it has nothing to do with the book.

– I'll bear that in mind.

The smile that follows is unconvincing. Nell opens the door, allowing the chill air from the hall in, undoing the work of the fire and considers saying something else, but Maman is making notes.

– Would you mind closing the door on your way out? *Suaimhneas.*

24

One night when Cleary stayed over, he revealed that he'd never heard the sound. Not everyone on the island could, which fascinated the climatologists and paranormal types who came here. Why one group and not another. No markers had been found, nothing that particularly predisposed one person over another in being able to hear it. Nell envied him. Being exempt from the thrum that thwarted the place. It doesn't hurt, but the rattle from chest to throat unnerves her each time.

They unfurl stories from the past. First love, school bullying, virginity. The music that saved your life. He likes these back-and-forths, the *I'll see your terrible haircuts and raise you a bad tattoo*. Nell rolls with it, a little less keen. She has always known the power of holding back. Not showing your hand.

On mornings after he stays over, she is up first, raking out the fire and warming the old range. In the garden, she picks chives for eggs. The wind is up, bending the trees while the kettle boils. She is due at Rathglas so will have to hurry him out of the house. Something her mother used to say, half-joke, half-warning floats up. *Never cook for a man, or you'll be doing it for life.* So many of her old lines. *The world is a big place outside of this postage stamp.* Nell has considered this literally. Parcelling herself into a box and mailing it around the world. So many of her new ideas are about being somewhere else.

She carries in a tray, with a plate and a mug of tea. The pillow is hitched up behind him, forearms folded over bare chest.

– Lovely, thanks. None for you?

– God no. Can't eat in the mornings. Never could.

She watches him shovel eggs in. There is no good time to ask, but he's vulnerable now, his arms darker than his chest and shoulders. Farmer's tan.

– I heard you were married before.

– Oh yeah? Not much to it. What do you want to know?

A coolness creeps in, but he doesn't shut down the question outright.

– What prompted it?

– Young. Stupid. Got swept up in it, I guess.

It's a surprise that he was so utterly headlong about it. Reckless even.

– I liked that she wasn't someone I knew, or *everyone* knew, or had seen around the town for years. I *liked* not knowing who her parents were, every drunk uncle. All her fucking aunties who'd be up the church lighting candles every hand's turn.

Nell pulls on jeans, hunts for her other trainer as he talks.

– I thought I'd go and live with her in the city. Change of scene and all that. Thing is, though, she really liked it here. Talked about it non-stop. Got all sentimental about the landscape the way all the eejits who don't live here year-round do. A sort of a switcheroo – she wanted to be here, I wanted to go there.

– But you were in love with her?

– I suppose … I think I was more in love with the idea of getting out of here.

– So what went wrong?

Nell knew. Everyone did. That they didn't get married here on St Stephen's Day, a custom of the island and its winter weddings. Instead, they opted for autumn, which some considered bad luck. The marriage only lasted a few months. They had split by the anniversary of their first kiss the summer after.

– There are no hard feelings, really. Good luck to her.

There is something in his face then. Not regret, but the thought forming that this rashness reflects badly on him. That he made poor choices and Nell will judge him for it.

– You're not a bit like her.

– I should hope not.

– Total opposite.

– Good to know. Listen … I have to go. C'mon. UP.

She makes a grab for the duvet and kisses his clavicle lightly.

– You really know who you are, Nell.

He says this quietly, without looking at her, fiddling with his watch.

– You do your own thing. You don't care if that shower in the town think you're a weirdo.

Nell stares. The red flag of 'weirdo'.

– I mean, I don't think that – Shit, sorry – that came out wrong.

– Don't worry. I learned a long time ago not to care what people here think of me …

– Good luck today, with the work … what is it you do out there anyway?

– I'm still figuring it out.

Watching him thread his belt, forearms moving, the sunken dip of his throat is a spell. She wants to climb back into bed. He senses it too, shifting back to polite, daytime chatter. He grabs his phone before planting a long kiss and disappearing.

On the road out to Rathglas, bike chattering on the lane, *weirdo* burrows in under her skin. That shower of Ryan's wasters can say what they like. Fuck 'em.

At the gates, she props the bike against the wall and opens her coat. Undoes the top three buttons of her top and scoops one breast out of her bra. Holding the phone above, she clicks.

By way of an apology for being nosy. She presses send.

25

Muireann descends the ladder down to the cove, which is stony and uneven. A small headland juts out, making the bay hard to find unless you know the island.

There are dull patches of sand, but not enough to entice anyone to lie down on it. Amid the rock-pool slime, limpets cling and tiny crabs scuttle. The water is always dark, because of seaweed. It's too dangerous to swim due to a vicious rip current and a hypothermic cold. Maman forbade it after an Iníon drowned a couple of years ago. She took it badly and the Iníons worried for her. That might have been the start of the distance. Of Maman spending less time among them. Markers bob on the surface, green flags for the lobster creels, red for the crab pots. A mini flotilla that cheers Muireann any time she sees them. With some luck, there'll be some brown crabs in the pot. She gathers seaweed that has washed up, other varieties have to be prised from the rocks. Pepper dulse – known as the truffle of the sea – can be used for cooking. Toothed wrack for baths.

Meal preparation is communal, and there is a division of labour – it is Muireann's job to grow things and oversee the fishing pots in the cove. She's less keen on cleaning but helps with the menu when Sadhbh allows it. It makes her happy to think of helping to feed everyone. Checking the pots, bringing down the rod some days, the feel of oily kelp. Mostly she likes the solitude. She taught some of the Iníons to fish, but they know to give her space. The cove is one of the few places for her to be alone. It's hard to pinpoint, but something has shifted up on the cliff. As if things were almost correct and proper, but off by a couple of inches.

Growing up in a big family makes loners of some. It's a long time since she's thought of the farm. The acid waft of slurry, wool snagged on the fence, her father's strong arms pulling a slick, bloodied calf out from its mother. Funny that she left one home full of people for another.

Eight or nine steps down the ladder, Rathglas disappears from view. It's a relief sometimes for it to be out of sight. To have a morning alone with the fish and whatever creatures have wandered into the creels and pots. Muireann likes to sit on the large boulders, rock smooth as sealskin. Fifteen feet out, on a flat plinth carved out by the sea, is the island's infamous stake. Imposing when the tide is out, the slim stone pillar dates back four hundred years, when island dissenters were tied to it and left to drown in the rising tide. From those who wouldn't pay tithes, to women accused of witchcraft, or adultery, it was used liberally. Muireann is convinced all this history is lodged in the column to this day. She preferred the bay when the tide is in, and the stake hidden beneath the water. It creeps her out. The frenzied kind of justice it represents.

There was a day, not long after she'd started setting the makeshift pots, when one of the creel lines snapped. The only option was to wade in after it. The tide came in faster, too fast it felt, and the line kept snaking away on the surface. With the water rising, she felt more uneasy, less surefooted on the stones now that she was waist-deep. An unexpected swell swept her feet from under her and then water was in her ears. Gasping, she surfaced, searching again for the rope. One more try and then she'd have to turn back. Another wave, her nose flooded, and she pushed herself up. That was when she heard it. Singing. The words were indistinct, but it was more than one voice. High, female, notes bending to an odd pitch. The next wave carried the rope to her, and she seized it, dragging the creel behind. By the time she was back on shore, feet grazed and breathless, the singing had stopped.

It might be a story Nell would want to hear. Muireann could at least tell her about the stake.

After the trays of fish are loaded up, Muireann scours the cove to see what the waves have thrown up. Driftwood and scraps of net. Things which she saves for Nell, depositing them like an offering outside the studio door. Today, she leaves a mermaid's purse, from a skate. Aisling had them all in stitches at the benches one day, speculating that the island men use them as sex toys. The laughter brought Maman to the window. Seeing her staring down, Muireann couldn't gauge her expression, but it filled her with the same feeling as before. An imperceptible change, the way the light fades here at night.

26

It was Cleary's suggestion to go to the pub. A sort of date. He wanted to talk about something, and she feared a lengthy backtrack over their last conversation. Ryan's wasn't just a pub. It was also partly a hardware shop that sold other random bits. It was possible to order steel wool and a pint of stout with the same tenner. Locals joked that Johnnie's spirit measures in the bar were so meagre it was prudent to buy a bottle of surgical spirits to top them up. Nell got soaked on the way in from Rathglas, under the evening's blanket of drizzle. Being early afforded a chance to eavesdrop on barstool banter. She's always liked the low rumble of chat. The wall-mounted television permanently on. Horse-racing. Melbourne, California, long sandy flats in Dubai.

At the bar, the men are discussing the merits of each-way bets and accumulators. Davey Lawlor from the boats is regaling the room with a story he loves to tell about the time one of the well-known online bookies rang to offer him a large sum to end his five-race accumulator when he was on race four. By race number three he was certain that Gurteen – a majestic Blood Bay – was the answer to all his problems. At this point in the story, Davey, as he does every time he tells it, dislodges himself from his stool, standing up like a boy band singer during a chorus. Puffing out his chest and warming to his punchline.

– An' I told those fuckers, 'STICK YOUR FUCKING MONEY UP YOUR HOLE!'

The story always ends with riotous laughter, multiple raised glasses and calls for another round. What Davey never says is that he lost that fourth race and ended up with nothing.

Since the wife conversation, Nell can't shake her annoyance that Cleary had listened to the talk about her in the town. It surprises her that the weirdo comment has gotten under her skin. The people who thought it are probably here. Slurping pints, waiting for her to pass and wink at each other. Not Murphy and the older pub gang. They are nothing but respectful, old-fashioned like that. It's the younger lads. All coked up and flinty.

Murphy cracks another gale of laughter just as Cleary walks in. Nell is partly obscured by a coat hanging on a hook. He hasn't seen her yet, and she likes this moment of watching him, before he's aware of her. Jaw angled in tension, the graphite eyes. For now, she forgets her irritation at the dig.

– Nell, hey.

The smell of cold sea air rising from him.

– How's it going? Pint?

– I'm grand. I'm going to get a short one myself.

It sounds formal, but this is new, being out in public. She has a sudden longing for a cigarette.

He returns from the bar and sits on the stool opposite instead of sliding into the banquette. It feels odd, the distance. There's no reason for him not to be beside her, his hand around the small of her back.

– How was your day?

– I had an idea for a new piece. About Banshla, where you gave out to me about swimming? I'm thinking of doing something down by that bit of the strand where the rocks end …

The lads at the bar have paid them no mind so far. On the TV, thoroughbreds at a Tokyo racecourse are galloping across the screen.

– I was thinking – you know those weird clamshells that always wash up there? The ones wi—

It's unconscious, dropping 'weird' in there. *I'm using weird, because weird is a normal thing to say, see?* That as words go, *weird is no big deal.*

Under the table, he places a hand on her thigh and glances up to check it's OK, an act she finds so moving. She is about to say this, but in a jokey, deprecating way, when he clears his throat.

– Listen, I meant to say this the last time at yours. I have to go away.

– Away?

– Yeah, reluctantly. Three weeks.

– I thought Davey and the lads came back every day?

– Yeah, they do, but I signed on for a spell on one of the bigger boats. With Liam Dooley. More money. I'm not a big fan of those harbour heads anyway.

She hadn't expected this. 'Reluctantly' is reassuring. 'Reluctantly' means he would rather stay, with her.

– That's a lot of time out on the water.

– You're telling me. My sea legs aren't even the best … Does it sound mad that I'm not great with water?

– Do you absolutely have to do it?

– I need the cash. You know what it's like here. There's only so many impotent bulls need incinerating. I applied to the rigs too. Just waiting to hear back. I could have worked with Pajo on the salmon farm, but it's not great out there. Some of those lads get badly injured.

– I get it. The only reason I give those tacky island tours is so I can eat. This year's been really bad with the weather. A rake of cancelled ferries, so I'm down a good bit money-wise. It's the only reason I took on the—

Maman's warning flits in.

– The job up at the convent?

– Yep. I'm spending a lot of time out there. But if I wasn't doing that, I'd still be an artist who cleans other people's toilets.

– Money. A total fucker. And on that cheery note, and I know we've only just sat down, but I've to go. Up at the crack of dawn. Last night of trying to get my lazy arse used to boat hours. But I wanted to see you, even for a bit.

He throws back the neat whiskey. Nell tucks away a pang of disappointment.

– You're going already?

– Have to. You have me worn out …

He winks and takes her hand.

– Seriously though, I'm wrecked and I've got to get some sleep training in. I'll give you a shout when I'm back, yeah?

– Sounds good. Be safe, you.

– And Nell?

– What?

– Send me some more of those photos …

– I'll see what I can do …

– It'll make long nights surrounded by other blokes quietly wanking or puking much easier …

They laugh and exchange a long kiss. One of the pasty regulars sitting at the bar sends up a salacious whistle. And then he is gone. Into the ink of the night. Nell wishes he'd warned her. Or stayed longer. Perhaps this thing between them has plateaued already. She orders one more glass of wine, opens her notebook and keeps writing. Scraps. A sketch of the clamshell idea. An hour later she is still there when Johnnie flashes the lights. The lamps on the wall wink on and off.

– Last orders, ladies and gents.

Outside, it's mild and without thinking her feet move along the road, inching towards his cottage. One last gaze in the window before he's gone.

The sitting room window is open. Laughter, two voices. Dodging around gas canisters and logs, Nell moves to the window, heart in mouth. There are cans of stout on the table. Someone sits opposite Cleary with their back to the window. Hunched over the coffee table, rolling a cigarette with concentration. Cleary watches, half bemused and drains a can.

– Give it here, ye dope.

The man passes the thin strip over, which looks flimsy, almost frugal.

– I'm away for a piss. Don't fuck that up! I'm out of papers. He pats Cleary's shoulder tenderly as he passes. Nell's smile fades when the man returns from the bathroom. Jimmy Cleary.

Jimmy sucks the smoke greedily and raises it aloft with his can. Not on the wagon then.

– To that old bitch, the sea. Don't you fucking drown on me!

They laugh like hyenas. Shrill, aggressive.

The disappointment she felt at him leaving her in the pub is subsumed by the kind gesture. One last check-in with his uncle. There is goodness in him. Feeling bittersweet under the moon, she moves off down the hill.

27

After these intense weeks, they know so much about each other and yet also virtually nothing. In a way, it suits her that Cleary was going. Her life has changed gear. The days seem to have fewer hours. But the thing pooling in her gut is unmistakable. A kind of saudade. Would it have been so hard to say that she would miss him? To offer him some words that might have comforted him out in the swells, stinking of brine.

Focus has been a long-term problem. It's a couple of years since she finished anything worth submitting to a gallery. Always chasing new things. After the Iníon book is done, she will head back out here to Greenawn and research another new piece. The finale will involve burying herself. Covering each limb with shells and seaweed. Whatever flotsam the sea discards. An alarming amount of manmade waste washes up on the island and the piece will address that too. But ultimately it's about death, but then art is always about death in the end.

The first night after he left, a brutal storm came. A gale mauled the trees, rattled the roof tiles and made music in the throats of all the chimneys. A theatrical performance of lightning came in angry forks. Large rocks were wrenched from the cliffs last winter and are now part of the sea. Acts of diminishment. The island getting smaller.

Nell listens through the night. Each sonic boom, every metal sliver cutting through the sky. The roof rattling as though being danced on. She and Cleary text back and forth and she doesn't envy him out there on the boat.

After a groggy sleep Nell cannot face Rathglas. She packs a few bits and heads to Cloughkeel beach to swim. The bay is the deepest point on the island. The water slate grey, rocks blackened by the waves. Fanning out on her back, the waves toss her, but she is careful to orient herself to the shore. Eyes closed but alert with all other senses. Cleary's texting started out sweet and ended with typos and a request for photos. He's lonely out there. The boats are brutal.

It's easier to be alone; to have no anchors. Still, she feels a slight pang at his absence, although he's barely away. *Don't start.* The inky water moves in pleats, and she realises she is too tired for swimming. Arms and legs start to feel heavy; her body has had enough of the water. Salt gathers in the cut on her heel and the smart of it spreads. It's time to get out but a wave covers her mouth and nose.

Spluttering, she pulls herself upright, regaining balance. Something brushes her skin. A stumble and now water in her ears, and the waves pulling at flesh, almost indecently. The shore must be further away, feet frantically searching for the seabed. But nothing rises to meet them, only the cold swirl of water. Another wave hits the back of her throat and, clawing at the surface, she is above, for a second, grabbing air into her lungs. She scans the waves for other swimmers but there is no one. Panicking now, she urges her body up, up, thrashing towards the shore.

Back on the shingle, exhausted, breath slowing. The only sound is the waves, moving in and out, washing the shore. Gathering up clothes, her feet move quickly over the stones and away from the sea.

PART TWO

28

Last month, a stranger came to live on the island. A famous actor. Everyone knows his name but pretends not to when they encounter him. In the mini-mart, people stare, and he smiles politely because he is rich and American. He is capable of a passable British accent. Does a decent job at a Russian bad guy. His Australian accent in one film became a viral meme, but he seems to work consistently and can pick and choose projects.

The actor claims that his mother was from here and he feels 'very in touch' with his roots. Occasionally, he is seen wearing a jumper traditional to this region; occasionally a flat cap if the weather requires it. He has taken up residence at the most imposing accommodation on the island, Greenawn Castle, and has been spotted walking his dog on the nearby beach. A small, pretentious breed that looks out of place beside the working dogs and hardy mutts of the island. The castle is rumoured to cost four grand a week to rent. It dates back to the 1840s, a sort of castle-meets-stately home, built for an aristocratic widow from the mainland. Constructed in the silvery stone common on the island, it has crow-stepped gables, turrets on each corner and a grey pantile roof.

There has been no talk of a film shoot locally, and he appears to be alone, moving around the town with the air of a man with a purpose. Not quite a swagger, but a gait that incorporates swagger. A hint of camp and something like curiosity, as if he would stop to talk to anyone.

Every woman on the island – from bored teenager to old knitting circle dears – notices him. Whispering in the main street, blushing from eyelash to nape. He is hard to look away from. Traditionally handsome. Smaller in person than on screen, the peacock quiff of his hair – now starting to grey – is unmistakable. His mouth more pinched, he is the owner of an arrowed jawline. No one dares approach him, as much as they want to. But there are whispers of conquests. The school secretary with the immaculate hair, a young widow that several of the island men have been sniffing around.

His presence has made the island women more aware of their bodies. Shoving back shoulders: breasts out, Spanxing in their stomachs or inhaling deeply in the absence of Lycra. No one could confirm if there was a wife or girlfriend in tow, even though he was once a mainstay of the tabloids. Back when he was still considered boyish, rakish. He has told one newspaper that he's here for the break. The change of pace. The islanders are happy to take his money.

29

Muireann has spent the day in the garden, harvesting what was ready. A rogue flower has sprung up near the greenhouse; blue, star-shaped. A tiny piece of sky in the dark soil. It is beautiful but has no purpose. Everything here has to have a purpose. Edible, or useful. What is it called? The name skittles around in her head but proves elusive.

On Tuesdays and Fridays, dinner is usually fish, depending on what's caught in the bay. Baked potatoes on Monday. Stew on Thursday. Sides of mash, carrots, green beans. Leftovers are judiciously repurposed. On Sundays, they roster scrambled eggs for small groups if the hens are on form. Muireann adds garlic, chard and onions. Her tomatoes are legendary: fat, squat, verging on sweet. There are bowls of salad, heaped with alfalfa, another of Muireann's knacks. The weather over the summer was all over the place and as a result the garden yielded fewer vegetables this year. Some things inexplicably spoiled in the greenhouse, and Sadhbh became a little less generous with portions.

On rare evenings, there is a cake, made from fruit about to turn, which arrives unceremoniously and is devoured. A tart made with plums from the orchard. Apple pie. But not recently. No birthdays are celebrated at Rathglas, which suits most. A reminder of old lives, of birth, of mothers.

Muireann's own mother would be seventy now; seventy-two, maybe? Everyone knew she used to lie about her age. Whenever they went to a do, or a wedding, Marie would sit for hours beforehand, in her underwear, making up her face. Terrified of getting powder on her one good dress because dry cleaning was such a luxury. Muireann would sit on the edge of the bed, the pink, frilled valence tickling the backs of her legs, and watch this ritual in awe. Lashes spidery and dramatic, her mother pouting as she applied layers of mascara. This was always the moment Muireann thought she transformed. From the woman who made the beds and dinners to some other glamorous figure. A quick O of lipstick – nothing as bold as red, rather a subtle, dusky shade. After her parents left, Muireann would practise this in front of the mirror with spittle on her lips. The next day her mother would lie in bed, curtains pulled until it was dark again, shouting for her cigarettes.

The blue flower. *Love-in-a-mist.* That was it.

– Muireann?

She's been so lost in recalling that blueness that she hasn't heard Sile approaching.

– Sister! Sorry. Daydreaming about flowers.

– Do you have a minute?

– Sure. Everything OK?

– Not here.

She jerks her head towards the building and the rows of windows. They move down the garden, past the beehives and around the back of the chapel.

– I don't … I hope I'm not speaking out of turn.

– OK. Well, get it off your chest, whatever it is.

– I know some of us can be opinionated, but evening assembly is important to so many of us.

– I think so too.

– So what will we do without it?

– What do you mean?

– Maman just told a few of us that she wants to get rid of it.

– She said that?

– Yes, in the dining room just now. Said that it was a distraction and led to arguments.

– Really? It has always seemed good-natured to me …

– She said it encouraged division and prideful behaviour.

Maman rarely attended the nights, so it's an even more inexplicable decision. Muireann can think of no reason for it.

– I really don't get it.

– Why would she take away something that everyone enjoys?

Muireann is tempted to respond with her first thought, that there is malice in it, but she pushes it away.

– Try not to worry, Sile. I'll see what I can find out.

On the walk back to the main building, Muireann broods. It's an odd move on Maman's part. Everyone looks forward to Wednesdays. But she knows it isn't really about the discussion night. There's something else. A tear in the fabric of how things have always worked.

30

It is early October and snails have gotten into the studio, leaving silver tracks around the legs of the desk. Nell had kept two as pets as a kid. She was heartbroken when raucous blackbirds pounced after she put them outside for some air.

With Cleary gone a fortnight, Nell makes the most of the reclaimed hours. When not at Rathglas she spends time researching the Greenawn burial project, gathering materials. It would be durational. Three days. Longer, depending on the weather. She could apply for funding, but thoughts of the process incite dread. Scrabbling for money just so that she can be the only thing she knows how to be. It would also mean she'd be committed to finishing it.

Nell is on her hands and knees, dabbing at the marks on the carpet with a rag, when she hears raised voices in the corridor. She stops to listen, holding her breath.

The old studio door hangs ajar, thanks to a handle she has tried and failed to fix. She moves towards the voices, one of which she recognises. The tone is unmistakably one of anger. If she is careless, she will be seen. Clinging to the wall, she inches her head out and listens.

Z and Sadhbh are arguing in the quiet way of hissed whispers. Sadhbh points, her face livid, shaking her head. Z holds something behind her back and the unwillingness to hand it over infuriates Sadhbh even more. She lunges, snatching it from her.

Nell, shocked, strains to see what, but the cook's back is turned.

– Don't ever do that again, Z.

Sadhbh stomps away, purple-cheeked. Nell steps back into the room and waits before softly closing the door.

She's heard of disagreements between the group but not of this kind. There's not enough time to ask Muireann about it if she wants to make the mini-mart before closing. The promise of a bottle of wine to go with dinner urges her out the door and into the evening.

* * *

Wavering over the purchase of a lemon for her fish, she finds only a pallid thing, its yellowness faded, the skin puckered. She's so absorbed in weighing up the discoloured peel that she doesn't notice the actor until she hears him asking for cigarette papers. His voice is possessed of that American twang of up-down notes. A slight drawl that he works hard to hide in interviews.

The shop doesn't stock his particular brand of cigarette papers, but he is polite in the face of it. Cathal, starstruck at the till, says he'll check the stockroom just in case. *Oh yeah, Cathal*, she thinks, *see if they have artichokes and a Geiger counter while you're at it.* His voice reminds her of places far away. Landscapes she'd like to see. All the possibility that comes with being from something bigger. Living near highways and rail-road crossings; three-lane motorways that lead to opera houses and canals and galleries.

Cathal makes a performance of loudly shoving boxes around in the back. The actor saunters the aisles, pausing to look at marine tat tourists buy. Anchor mug racks, fish clocks, plastic lighthouses that look worse under the lights tonight. Nell engages in her own pretence of rummaging while extending a discreet side-eye. She watches him pick up a set of candles; gaudy-looking peach things. He tests the tension in a fishing rod – his fingers slim, precise – before picking up a six-pack of water.

– Ryan's down the road will sell you a five-litre bottle. Cheaper. Less plastic too.

He eases the bottles back on to the lower shelf. Turning, he flashes that trademark expression everyone has seen him do. A trying-not-to-smile grin, which of course renders him even more attractive. It reminds Nell of a yellow road sign. *Danger*, it says. In one of his films – a big-budget, critically panned period drama – one critic wrote that his mouth had looked out of place in a formal Edwardian drawing room.

– That's good to know. Thank you.

He doffs the flat cap he's wearing with exaggerated politeness.

– Hi, I'm Nick.

Nell feels an overwhelming urge to laugh, because this is surely the most redundant introduction in the world. Everyone knows who he is. Instead, she smiles wanly, stretches out her hand and offers a polite, 'Nell'.

– Ah, finally. Cathal here was telling me that if a person wants to get to know the island, you're the one to ask.

– Did he now …?

She knows what he means, but it feels good to pretend that she doesn't. She likes that on some banal level he was aware of her before this moment.

– Do you still give tours? To visitors …?

– I do. Sometimes. But we're heading in to off-season now. Less demand.

The haughtiness came out unexpectedly. There is no reason to be this way with him.

– That makes sense.

Neither of them moves. He inhales deeply as though smoking a slightly wretched cigarette.

– Have you ever done any, say, one-to-one arrangements, you know, for the right fee?

Before the final word emerges from his movie-star mouth, he realises how it sounds.

– Wait. I didn—

– FOUND SOME! With impeccable timing, Cathal emerges from the stockroom, hand in the air, clutching the papers like a winning lottery ticket. He trots them, puppy-like, to the actor, who accepts them without lifting his eyes from Nell.

She flicks her hair and attempts what she hopes is a coy laugh.

– It's fine, I think I got your meaning ... you'd like a private tour of the island, yeah?

Cathal shuffles back to the till, a little wounded.

– Exactly. I'm still finding my way around ... but I can pay whatever you think is a suitable fee for your time and any inconvenience.

It wouldn't take him long to find his own way around the island. Figure it out from north to south. Maybe he's not on firm ground, away from his usual life, his confidence leaking a little.

Nell wants to dispel any suggestion that she's keen to show the film bigwig around. She takes her time, thinking idly on his pronunciation. SEM-EYE instead of semi.

– Oh! I'll be back in one tick ...

She leaves him standing near the till and rushes down an aisle as if urgently searching for something. Shampoo, cotton wool, a comb for a new piece of work. She hovers in the aisle, out of view. TOM-AY-TOE. LEE-SHURE. BAY-SIL.

Throws in an extra carton of milk. Chocolate. More wine.

Cathal is stuttering about some film, attempting to impress the actor, who looks around, trying to find Nell. She waits another beat and emerges, casually, breezy.

– I'm working in the morning, but could do this Wednesday afternoon?

– That works.

That dangerous smile. Lethal.

– Say 2 p.m.? We can't leave it any later – it gets dark early here.

For a moment, he looks hesitant. Perhaps it's the mention of darkness, of night.

– Sounds like a plan. Where should we meet?

– How about outside here?

– Sure. See you Wednesday.

At the till, in gratitude, he insists she go ahead of him. Gingerly, she unloads her basket, suddenly self-conscious about the wine, a cheap €7 bottle. Back in the US he probably lives beside a vineyard. Maybe even part-owns one with some other celebrity friends. Knows all about grapes and microclimates and tannins. *Turbidity.* A word she read once in a wine column and thinks about all the time. There is a loveliness to soil. The dampness. Secrets in all its molecules. The insects and crumbling peat. The feeling that one day it will hold her body. When they were still oversharing, firing stories back and forth, Cleary had told her he wanted to be cremated. Nell disagreed. She wants to be wrapped in layers of dank earth – all those dark nutrients – to let every creature feast on whatever is left of her.

She is loading up the basket on her bike when he leaves the shop. Leans up against the coal and briquette stand. One-handed, he works away on a rollie, fingers working as if sifting flour. A practised gesture that suggests ease and nonchalance.

A wink, as he sparks it up and turns to move up the hill.

Nell feels a slight rush. The lit tip of the cigarette moving away from her in the dark. *No,* she says to herself. *Cut it out.*

That night, after the salted fish, it takes two gins – two and a half, to be precise – before Nell types the actor's name into a search engine. Then various film sites, sifting through newspaper interviews, checking his age. In the search box, his name autocompletes to 'married'. The more recent ex-wife she knew about, but there was a first one. A late teenage marriage to a co-star.

She does a trawl of blind gossip sites for the real dirt. Full of affairs and secret abortions and ludicrous coke habits, but also stories of predators, murderers and paedophiles. There are no stories about him, except one, about possibly fucking an actress in a toilet at an awards ceremony.

By the third drink Nell has illegally downloaded his last film, in which he plays a young widower. Vulnerable and afraid of getting hurt, he slowly falls for a café owner who teaches him about love and redemption. More searches reveal he has children with three different women. And then she finds it, a pretentious film journal interview in which he talks about the spirits that guide his work. How he regretted turning down an auteur director who died months later and that his process centred on 'channelling the lives of his ancestors'.

Oh god. He's going to talk her head off about 'coming home', like every second tourist off the ferry.

Nell throws back the gin and replays the clip, watching him splayed and moving over the actress on the couch. She puts the laptop aside, removes her nightshirt and arranges herself on the bed, mimicking the *oh yes* position of the actress. The angle is hard to capture with the phone, but after several attempts, she finds it and snaps. She looks at her own face, the image more haunted than erotic. But Cleary out there, swirling on the waves, will appreciate it.

31

Muireann answers the buzzer to the main gate and suggests they skip the usual route to the studio through the main door. Instead, she guides them around the side of the house, to a gate tucked into the garden wall.

– Where are we going? I need coffee or water or—

– Detour. Consider it phytotherapy.

There is an upward lilt, a hint of musicality in the way she says this.

– Are you allowed to say where you're from?

– I thought you weren't supposed to be asking us all too many questions?

They laugh, moving along a lane shaded by trees and shrubs, emerging at the back end of the garden. On the left are clusters of beehives, stacked like fruit palettes. Beyond them, the chapel is to the right. In between are the greenhouses and compost heap. The oily stink unsettles Nell's stomach.

One greenhouse is filled with courgettes, kale and spinach, a leafy shrine to vitamin E. Gliding past rows of pristine produce, Muireann follows Nell's eye.

– Still haven't figured out a humane way to kill the

bastard slugs, so the greens are in here. Rocket, chard. All the lettuces.

On a large table dusted with soil, Nell spots the orchids. An elegant army in white and pink. The air is a mix of good and unpleasant smells attempting to cancel each other out.

Muireann adds compost to the orchids' roots.

It's not unlike Nell's own obsessive growing. Plants and herbs for skin balms or pessaries for women who need them. The seed-bedding, the carefully nurtured slips and cuttings, the windshields she constructed to keep the sea gales from stymying the roots. It's the process. Not unlike art, in a way. Putting your hands in the soil – reaching into the earth – steadies her. When she is hung-over, Nell plants and weeds. Loosening the roots of her seedlings and giving them a new home in the ground.

– This way – watch your step – I want to show you something.

Nell follows behind on the uneven path. Behind greenhouse C is a small shed, out of place in the well-tended garden. Inside, Muireann moves around flipping switches, but Nell knows before the lamps come on what this is. The deep green smell of it, pungent.

– Weed? Really?

She laughs.

– Personal use. Medical. If we run out of provisions, we'll always have this to distract us.

– I wondered about that. Is there enough food to go round?

– Mostly. I manage to grow a lot. And there's whatever we can get from the sea. But if the summer is not great, and this past one wasn't, it can get a bit lean. There are also more of us here than there used to be.

– Maybe you could supplement the food budget selling this stuff? You'd make a killing. Set yourselves up so you're all not living off dandelion soup, or whatever.

– Maman would never allow it. Even if she did, there'd be the small matter of having to post stuff. We're not— well, we're not *barred* from going into the town.

– But it's strongly discouraged. Especially if you're hawking spliff.

– Something like that. We don't go into town unless it's an emergency. Just makes it easier – cleaner – Maman thinks.

For a moment Rathglas feels like the loneliest place in the world. All this weed would certainly help. Muireann pulls a pouch from her smock and rolls a joint with brownish paper.

– Where do you get skins if you don't go near the town?

– They're hemp. I make them.

Nell is impressed by the self-sufficiency. Muireann pauses to run her tongue along the edge.

– Were you always a smoker? Before here?

– Yeah, but I used to mix it up with booze and that didn't go so well for me. Part of my problem is that I don't sleep and they both helped. Until the drink didn't.

– I can bring you a tea I make for insomnia. Been making it for years. Cathal in the mini-mart says it has the same effect as being hit on the head with a blunt object.

– Sounds great. I used to live for blackouts.

Muireann inhales slowly, holding the smoke deep in her lungs, allowing the drug to do its work.

– So what are you working on when you're not here? What kind of art?

She passes the joint to Nell, and the smoke hits her throat like a dart. The effect is welcome, a warm wave moving up each arm and into her chest.

– A lot of the work is outside, on land, in forests. I can't separate place from the ideas, or the thing I end up creating.

– An island sounds perfect for that; you get to cover a lot of ground.

– In a way, but then there's the risk of getting stuck. I've associated art with the island for so long that I feel like I'm doomed to keep making versions of the same thing.

– But lots of artists do that, right? Create the same thing over and over?

– There's this German artist, Peter Dreher. He painted the same glass of water repeatedly. More than five thousand times. Said it worked because he could find a way to see it afresh each time. I get that. I never look at Banshla the same way twice.

– So your glass is the island?

– No. If anything, I think my glass is my body, as in my body as it inhabits the space around it … which happens to be here.

– And one informs the other – is that it?

– This is going to sound utterly insane, but I feel like part of my body *is* the island. As if the stones on the beach are embedded in my heels ... or that in some corner of my lungs there is also sea air and saltwater. I guess I feel as though my body is an extension of the island, and all of nature in a way, and ... and oh my god, I've clearly smoked too much of this stuff. Sorry for the boring art lecture.

Muireann throws her head back and lets out a throaty cackle.

– I was quite enjoying that, actually. No one talks like that in here.

Nell lies down on the shed floor, her mind spreading out. All she wants to do is touch the orchids. She has a sudden image of her mother. The elder tree that used to stand outside her window. Cleary saying *weirdo*. The lighthouse beam slowing right down. She thinks she can hear singing, but it might be the shrill notes of the wind running through the outbuildings.

She likes Muireann. Too often, women compete. God knows Nell had seen it in the art scene. Networkers, plagiarists, users. At this moment, the herb spooling through her blood, the tingle of it feels good. They pass the joint back and forth until her head feels heavy. If she were to sit up now, she might be weighed right down, chin touching her thighs.

Muireann begins to gather up the skins and matches, indicating work to be done. Nell lingers, cross-legged.

– How do you get on with Maman?

A basic question, delivered with impeccable neutrality. Muireann stares at the floor.

– Fine. She's ... become a little concerned about being in charge. She used to be more laid-back, even keel, maybe, but now she seems ... I dunno ... intent on asserting more authority. And I hate clashes or politics, I just want an easy life. But I guess the pagan in me is down with her head-witch vibe ...

Muireann smiles and her mouth is all moon again as she offers Nell an arm up.

– But she's definitely a mother figure for us. Lots of people here were – maybe are still – a little lost. They look up to her. They want to feel looked after, as well as being part of something.

– 'Was'?

– IS ... I just don't know if everyone feels the same about her anymore.

– What's brought it on?

– It's not any one thing ... well, maybe one particular thing ...

– Which is?

Muireann flicks the ash away and nods at Nell.

– You, for one.

She purses her lips and expels a plume of smoke.

– Me?

– Uh-huh ...

– I get it. But I've got to tell you – when the letter arrived, it really sounded like a group invite. And then when I got here ... it was clear that wasn't the case.

– Look, no one hates you. Well, maybe Rose ...

She laughs.

– It was just ... we always made decisions together and this seemed to be one that she just made herself and didn't think to tell anyone.

– I wish I'd known.

– How could you have? That said, there was always going to be friction with a total stranger landing ... you're the first outsider allowed here in thirty years.

– I'm sorry me being here has caused shit.

– It's not you. Honestly. It's on her.

Muireann stubs the butt out and gets to her feet.

There's a ... I don't know. I'm probably overthinking it. Thank you, drugs! C'mon, I'll walk you to the studio.

She hauls Nell up, who dusts off the floor grit, feeling a soft heaviness in the back of her head.

Back in the studio, Nell reads through more of the testimonies. Maybe it's the weed, but the stories land harder. Suddenly, she feels stupid for coming here, knowing that the invitation wasn't universally extended. It's too late to back out now. A wave of tiredness and deflation hits and she opens the window for air. She lies on the studio floor, listening to the sea below, casting waves in and out.

32

In the bunk, Cleary's stomach heaves. That night's dinner dances in his guts. Potatoes, peas, overdone pork chops. Distraction is what's required when the sea churns the boat. On his phone, he clicks on a picture of Nell.

It was taken secretly, while she was sleeping. The pale orb of her shoulder, the knotted path of spine. He probably should have asked but didn't want to risk waking her. Her skin moved him unbearably. It was hard for him to explain. Like being told a sad story.

The lads hung around in the small canteen after dinner to play cards. The rules say it's a dry boat, but one of the Latvian guys has a secret stash of rum. The thought of drinking rotates his stomach further.

He'll be back on the island soon. To routines, and the damp cottage, to pints in Ryan's. And to her. An unasked-for magic. He likes looking at her in bed. Throwing her leg across him and making jokes. Always reading. During the night, he would reach his arm across the sheets to find her. It was like reaching land.

33

It is raining heavily at Rathglas, the slow opening of the clouds, water tinkling in the gutters. Nell has been writing all morning and is finally starting to see the book's shape. There is a knock at the door, and Aurora has brought tea. Rather than hand it over as usual, she lingers. Fair-haired and pale, Nell would never have guessed she's Italian.

– Is there anything I can help you with, Nell?

– No thank you, but I really appreciate the tea. My throat is always a bit off in the mornings.

Aurora steps into the room anxiously. She stares at the materials on the table. The pile of folders.

– How are you doing, Aurora? I haven't seen you since … well, that day on the stairs.

– I'm sorry about that. My emotions get the better of me sometimes. The other Iníons tease me a little for being so soft.

She smiles at Nell and takes something from her pocket.

– I wanted to show you something … to explain.

It's a photograph of a town, taken on a sunny day. The sky is blindingly blue, with mountains in the distance. On the street are restaurants and cafés with tables and colourful awning. Men in groups smoking. A woman stands beside a white granite memorial. Nell squints at the structure, which contains rows and rows of names, chiselled in gold.

– Can you tell the names are only of men? Hundreds of them, some no more than boys. Young fathers leaving children behind.

– Where is this?

– Where I'm from. A tiny village in the mountains. This is the main square.

– It looks beautiful. Idyllic.

Nell has often longed to go somewhere like this. Wide, warm squares. The cool air of churches. Anonymity.

– It really is. I miss it so much. It holds a very rare record. One of the only villages where no men came back after the war. Not one. Every day on my way to school I passed this memorial and tried to imagine what it was like for the anxious wives. Waiting for a telegram. At the start of the war, some of the women were pregnant. There were children who never met their fathers, and fathers who never even knew they were to become fathers. When the end of the war was declared, the priest insisted the church bell was rung for a full day and night to mourn them.

Nell gestures to the woman in the photograph. Olive-skinned, deep furrows in her brow.

– Is this your mother?

– Yes. Violetta. Her father never came back. I never understood why she wanted her photo taken in front of it. A monument to grief and violence.

– That's so sad.

Aurora smiles but her eyes are filling up.

– But then I'm a total hypocrite.

– What do you mean?

– Here I am telling you about these heartbroken women, waiting for their husbands, their sadness and grief ... and I did the same thing! Coming here and never going home to her.

– You can always go back, can't you? Go and see her?

The tears Aurora has been holding back run down her face.

– I can't – she died last year.

– Oh god. I'm so sorry for your loss.

– Sometimes I think I won't get over the fact that I'll never see her again.

Aurora stares at the photograph. Nell hands her the undrunk cup of tea, which she accepts.

– It's not just about her being gone, never being able to see her, or call her one more time. It's ...

A sob catches in her throat.

The bell for dinner rings. Aurora's face crumples, reddened with tears.

– She became ill so suddenly ...

– Did you go back to Italy to see her when you heard she was sick?

Aurora shakes her head.

– No. I couldn't.

– Why?

– When I asked permission to go back, to be with her at the end, I was told it wasn't appropriate.

– I don't understand. Maman said *no?*

Aurora nods. Nell is incredulous.

– I'm an only child. When I think of her dying, calling out for me, I'll never forgive myself …

Aurora weeps convulsively. Nell moves to put an arm around her.

– Surely she could have made an exception?

– Maman said that it would break our vow of solitude. That I would be 'tainted' by the outside world. And that I had to think of the other Iníons.

Nell cannot believe the lack of compassion.

– Why didn't you just go anyway? I know I would have.

– You don't know what it's like here.

– Why not just walk out of the gate?

Aurora smiles bitterly.

– Because I don't have my passport.

– Why?

– When you arrive here, you have to hand over those kinds of things. Passports, ATM cards, driving licence …

Nell cannot speak. The dinner bell sounds again, and Aurora moves towards the door.

– I don't know what to say, Aurora. That's horrendous.

– I must go, I'm supposed to help Sadhbh set the table – and I've taken up too much of your time already.

After she shuts the door, Nell stands at the window for a long time, trying to absorb this. There is something horrifying about it. A needless cruelty. Did the other Iníons object at the time, or challenge Maman? Surely they must have rallied around Aurora in her time of grief. If they did not, it doesn't bear thinking about. In extricating themselves from a world of rules and judgement, it seems the Iníons have only found more in here.

She opens the window for air, suddenly glad to be meeting Nick later. Grateful for some other company. A distraction. Outside, clouds thicken in grey gluts. A gull soars past the window, emitting a high plaintive cry.

34

When she arrives, Nick is already outside the mini-mart. On the walk he tells her about his last job, shot in a small dry town, with an illegal shebeen and a community-wide meth habit. Unemployment was high, people were bored. It sounds a little like the island to Nell, without the meth. Mushrooms. Weed. The occasional shipment of pills consumed upstairs in Ryan's. Tourists are obsessed with the idea that the next stop from here is America. She always points in that direction on the tours, with a practised wistful glance towards the thin seam of horizon. Sometimes, when they've all gone back to the boat, she laughs about the tweeness of this faux film scene. The lone outsider on the cliff. Camera artfully picking up the waves crashing on the rocks below, with her as a wistful, wind-blown colleen.

Just as the red and white daymarks of the lighthouse come into view, the real reason for the walk is revealed.

– I know you bring people to the lighthouse – do you ever bring them out to see the Iníons?

The Iníons. That's not quite the word she expected to end that question. If he'd said Hegemony, or Desideratum

or Cunt, she would have arched a brow, but this ... is quite
sly. Well-played, even.

– Who told *you* about the Iníons?

He displays his practised pout.

– I read a *New York Post* article—

– Oh please! If I had a fiver for every gullible fool who
wandered off the ferry looking for that vision of this place.
That piece was pure rubbish. Insulting, too.

– I thought it was very interesting. Respectful. I lik—

– Apart from all the inaccuracies about the island, it made
the Iníons sound like a cabal of man-haters. A crazed cult
who dance naked, smeared in seaweed paste and period
blood.

The Iníons had not been the sole focus of the article about
modern isolated communities, but there were several sensa-
tionalist paragraphs about them that betrayed a barely
concealed scorn for their way of life. Suppositions about
their motivations and beliefs. The journalist implied that
they were an antique collective of batshittery. Queer, ritual-
loving communists. There was a drone photo of the chapel
and Muireann's well-tended garden. The weed shed could be
seen too, not that anyone would have guessed its purpose.

– Those women sounded fascinating to me ... just so ...
great.

– Great? Jesus! They're not a fucking band.

– I just ... I ... really admire their principles is all.

– That article made a joke of them. They keep to themselves and harm no one. It made them sound unhinged.

– The film world is crazy different these days. It's changed. Lord, I've changed. I'm already getting sent daddy roles … and I know the grandpa ones are probably not far behind.

Oh yes. She'd seen that one set in a New England seaside town where he was a sexy DILF who had a fling with his predictably volatile French neighbour.

– I feel like it's time for a change, you know? When I read that piece, it seemed like a sign. So I started taking notes.

– For what?

– I want, well, what I'd like to *try* and do is to make a documentary about the Iníons.

Of course, Nell saw it now. Magazine articles got optioned all the time. Film companies throwing down money for 1,500 words of copy about real people who likely had no say in the matter. People who might not have granted their permission to the profile in the first place. The Iníons hadn't invited that journalist to hold up their lives to the world. Even the islanders respected their choice to live in isolation. On some level, they understood that was the point of Rathglas: exile as a kind of self-preservation.

– You didn't want a tour at all.

– No, I did. Really.

– My role is less tour guide and more brain-you-want-to-pick – have I got that right?

– I really did want a tour. But I thought you could also tell me abo—

– Listen. I'm not being difficult, but people here leave the Iníons alone. Everyone else should too. I'm sorry, I just thought you wanted to see the island.

– It wasn't my intention to be sneaky or deceptive, I swear. I genuinely want to know all about this place. I bought a load of books, have been researching for months. I want to do this properly, considerately and with their cooperation only. What I'd really like is to find a way to talk to them. I don't know if they would be open, but it's worth a shot.

Nell can't look at him and focuses instead on Davey Lawlor's trawler scything across the bay.

– Look, think it over and, for now, let's do the tour. Give me your best tour spiel and no hard feelings. Deal?

Nell had said yes to the Iníons out of curiosity. Now that she's gotten to know the women, part of her feels protective of them. They'd all have their own opinions on this, but she's certain that many wouldn't like this intrusion.

His hand dips into his chest pocket for the tobacco pouch and Nell walks slightly ahead, beginning the well-rehearsed talk. Of how the lighthouse was built in 1881 and has a rare kind of Fresnel lens. That the cupola was blown clean off in the great storm of 1902. How it was originally meant to have 113 steps, but this was considered unlucky, so they added an extra one, to make 114. Thousands of times she has rolled through this, carefully hammered into shape, a nugget of metal. When she finishes, he applauds.

– Would it be OK for me to buy you a drink as a thank-you?

He moves closer, under the light of the beam.

– I suppose so. We can go to Ryan's, but I'm not sure you're ready for it.

– Sorry, I should have said – not tonight – I have a call with my agent. Maybe tomorrow night?

Slight disappointment tips over in her gut.

– Let's skip Ryan's and say the little hotel. The Cove Inn. Just down from the mini-mart. Would eight work?

– Sounds like a great plan. And again, thank you, Nell.

She watches him face into the wind, which scoops up his collar. The tour was a likely ruse. He's more than capable of making his own way around, but maybe he'd heard she was working with the Iníons. It's hard to keep anything a secret on the island.

35

October has dug itself in. A badger sett of long, grey hours. The wind is up most days, frosting the windows at Rathglas with salt. Blight has spoiled some of the autumn fruit. The greenhouse vegetables have also been slow to yield. At mealtimes, there are invocations to Danu. *If I get one more sniff of incense, I'm starting a riot.* The words drift in through the studio window one morning. It's complicated. An act of intervention, bringing supplies from the cottage garden, or from the mini-mart in the town, might cause offence. Maman would very likely not want her to interfere, and Nell does not want any strife. Muireann has explained that food is a concern and that they'll have to take precautions for the long winter ahead.

So it's not wholly unexpected when, after dinner, Sadhbh tells the group that rations will be introduced from next week. Two meals a day instead of three. Breakfast will be served closer to lunchtime and the next meal will be dinner in the evening. As cook, Sadhbh has been given the grim task of delivering the news. Standing at the head of the table, she tries to do so calmly, but it's hard to fully cover her dismay. This has been decided in everyone's interest due to a likelihood of future shortages in the colder months, she explains.

The group gasp. Rose swears, and unease spreads. Someone drops a plate. Ebele's chair shrieks as she stands up.

– Decided by who? This hasn't been discussed.

– I'm just the messenger, Sisters, but Maman always knows what is best for us.

– But we don't eat much as it is.

Sile's voice rises from among the rows of smocks.

– She's always watched over us, hasn't she? This is what she believes will get us safely through a long winter.

– Now hang on, I know things are tight but we've enough food, haven't we?

Muireann is on her feet, colour rising.

– And we always stockpile?

Aisling joins Muireann now.

– Everyone knows we can get by on soup in the cold months. It doesn't make any sense?

The other Iníons look at each other, alarmed.

– What's really going on here, Sadhbh?

Muireann squares up to Sadhbh, who will not hold her gaze.

– Nothing, I was just told to let you know …

Aisling and others join Muireann.

– And she couldn't come and tell us herself? That's really not on. I'm going to have this out with her.

Aisling stalks into the hall and can be heard taking the stairs two at a time.

The others sit back in their chairs despondently. Muireann's head is in her hands.

– Let's talk to her tomorrow. It's always about consensus, right, Muireann?

– Sadhbh, you and I know more about the food situation than anyone. Can't we just change up the meals a bit?

Aisling barges in, more angry now.

– She's not answering the door.

– Of course she's not. She doesn't want to face us.

Rose looks as if she might march up the stairs and bang down the door until it opens. Sadhbh, sensing this, puts a placatory hand on Rose's arm.

– I should have said: Maman has a headache. That's why she asked me to update you all on this.

Rose and Aisling exchange a look. For the first time that she can remember, Muireann feels a kind of dissent in the room. An unruliness.

36

At exactly the time the Iníons were dealing with this food crisis, Nell and the actor were leaving the Cove Inn. Nick wanted to see the lighthouse at night, stand under the beam in the dark and soak it up. They abandoned their drinks and set out.

Now, leaning into the slanting rain, he insists on hearing more stories of the island's history, of the lighthouse itself.

The rain deposits pebbles of water on her skin. The waves kettle-drum the caves under the cliff. They're almost there when the wind gusts, taking her hat with it, tumbling towards the cliff. He bolts after it, an utterly comic act. She shouts at him to leave it. It's cheap. There's another one in a drawer at home in a similar colour. This level of pursuit feels unnecessary, but she can't leave him out there alone, a plastic bag in a storm. Each time he catches up, bending to retrieve it, the wind snatches it again. Two gulls coast on the gust and Nell has an urge to see the scene from above. A bird's-eye view of this unfolding calamity. To circle with rain-slicked wings, puzzled by the game below. He gets too near the cliff edge, utterly focused on the hat, unaware of the distance. She runs jaggedly into the wall of rain, her shouts indecipherable in the wind. Nell lurches forward into the scutch grass and grasps his arm. The ground rises to meet them. A sopping bed of muck and stones. He laughs, possibly from the shock of it, grabbing her hipbone as they get up, steadying himself. Despite the rain, they are both laughing now. Muck smeared across the arse of their coats. The gin causing her to sway. He holds tight to her, the muddied hat clutched victorious in his hand. Clinging together, they stumble away from the cliff edge. The air is wild.

At the foot of the lighthouse, she begins the ritual: jiggling the key in the rusted lock, leaning her weight on the iron door, opening it into the dark. The smell rising. Of mould and seawater. The single bulb fizzes irritably to life and she beckons him to follow her up the steps.

When her mother died, she came up here a lot at night. Staring into the beam, to rattle the numbness. Blinding herself in small, incremental bursts. There was comfort in the light. The regularity of the sweep was a reminder that time passes; that you eventually move further away from pain into the future. The white shaft on the waves seemed to offer some kind of continuity, picking out the rocks.

Their feet echo, slightly out of time on the stone. Up they go, guided by her phone, until the final turn. She watches his reaction as they reach the lantern room. The light whirls – she's used to it – but he is transfixed by the Fresnel glass, angled and glossy. Nell opens the door out to the gallery rail and the wind is really raging now.

– Whoa. The sound of it. Imagine what it was like here a hundred years ago.

– There was a lightkeeper's wife here at that time who was a famous fortune teller. People came from the mainland in droves to see her.

– Did she read palms?

– And tea leaves. She was also a big believer in xenomancy.

– Which is …?

She closes the door, watching him on the opposite side of the lens.

– Divination by a stranger. The first person you meet on a Sunday, for example. The Greeks used to think that an accidental meeting with a shepherd was unlucky.

– Historically, these kinds of meetings were much worse for men.

He moves closer. The beam sweeps back and forth, the mechanics humming.

– Is that so …

He is beside her, staring intently. It's impossible to look away.

– Are we strangers?

There is no space between them now. Her colour rises.

– I don't know … I …

It happens quickly, the kiss. Breathing elevated, all oscillations. Discarding layers made heavier by the rain. Their movements intent and singular. He knows what he's doing. She likes the noises he makes.

And after, rolling in like a wave, she already wants that feeling again. The one of just before, before mouths on bodies and heat, before the actuality of what just happened. She lives for it, that wide bay of uncertainty, of going out on a limb.

Out there on the waves below, a container ship is trying to turn. It will take hours. There are no sharp left or right turns, only patience and skill.

37

The next morning, when the light outside is starting
to change, the actor has already left. Blue evicting the
black. *Uhtceare.* An old word for this feeling, early in the
morning. Nell makes tea and spots a note on the mantelpiece.

Let's try Ryan's tonight, same time? She smiles and sends
a text, gathers a notebook and an apple and sets off down
the track as the sun blinks open.

At the gates, the familiar line of the roof is grey against
the sunrise and the building has never looked bleaker. An
echo of an old workhouse, yet oddly beautiful in the light.
The studio is freezing, the sun hasn't made its way in yet.
The stove needs cleaning out, the remnants of old ash and
coal. By the door, there's a note in Muireann's hand on the
floor.

Come down to cove at 2pm.

Out in the garden, she looks out over the bay and thinks
about Cleary out there. Wondering when he's coming back.
Sometimes, she watches the boats returning. The men
relieved to be standing on the solid stone of the harbour,
stretching limbs. After a week of queasy swells and basic

meals, a swift decampment to Ryan's for baskets of chips and a feed of pints.

There are eyes on her back. Turning, she finds Maman watching her from the upper floor.

From the clifftop, everything is possibility. The impressionistic horizon is blurred by cloud. Few people have seen this side of the island, in a landscape where everyone knows every blade and stone. Twenty-five years ago, when she was a child, Christy Mullins, an old friend of her father's, used to bring them out this way in his boat. The Iníons would have been here by then. She remembers the thrill of the boat trip but no mention of a group of women living up on the cliff. The feeling of sheer exhilaration out on the waves. Chicken sandwiches sweating in clingfilm and a shared flask of tea.

On the shingle below, Muireann is emptying the traps. It is tricky work, but she is quick with her hands. Today she looks tired and off-colour.

– Hey there, I better be quick. Maman saw me in the cliff garden and will think I'm skiving off.

The crabs skitter, and Muireann grabs at their shells, transferring them to a damp sack.

– She seems to watch everything these days.

Muireann drops the sack and two of the crabs crawl on to the sand.

– FUCK.

Nell scoops them up quickly and helps keep the bag upright.

– How are you doing, anyway?

– Sorry for dragging you all the way down here. You just never get a minute up there.

She nods up towards the dark brick of the old convent.

– I'm glad of the break – it gets so bloody stuffy in that room with that weird heater. I was in early anyway.

– How's the book going?

– There's still a good bit to do. I think Maman might have been trying to write some sort of history herself but gave up.

– Which is where you come in.

– It seems so.

– Did she …

Muireann trails off.

– What?

– Is that really all she wants?

– I think so. What else could she want?

Waves slurp at their feet. Muireann resets the pots and walks to the ladder. They haven't known each other very long, but Nell can tell there's something off.

– What is it you think she wants?

– Don't mind me, it's just a feeling …

– How so?

– I mean, I – more than most of the others – understand the food thing. The rations. But it's not just that.

– How do the others feel?

– Some are happy to just plod along. Mutual respect was always key and a laid-back kind of ethos, for sure – but it feels like we're heading down the road of politics and bullshit. And no one wants an argument. In fairness, it's a tough job keeping things going, but ... it just feels ... I don't know. Not the same.

In the water below, the flash of a small fish.

– It's not for me to get involved, but I hope me coming here hasn't got something to do with this.

– It's not ... well, not your *fault*, but you being here makes it easier to implement change. Does that make sense? And this whole thing only works if everyone is on the same page, at the same time.

Nell gets it. If the women don't stick together, the whole structure will be in danger of falling apart.

Muireann ties the sack to her back, readying herself for the climb up. Nell can hear the crabs, the clack of their dark shells.

– Recording the history, I'm fine with. I just don't want any details of my life in there. The whole point of being here for me, for Aisling ... for most of us, is anonymity, silence, peace.

– I don't think Maman wants to betray that. The book is for all of you. It's a legacy.

– No disrespect to what you're doing, Nell, but I don't get this need to catalogue our lives. We could just live, be ... why the historical urge to 'capture' it?

– Look, I make art that by its very nature is totally ephemeral. I'm the last person to ask about permanence, but I can also see the flipside. That it's important to preserve the testimonies in some way.

– You've seen them?

– Only because Maman wanted me to get a sense of the people here, not just the buildings and land, or what the Iníons believe in.

Muireann stares at her, taking this in.

– She always said the testimonies were an unburdening. A way of casting off our old lives before starting a new one here. And she insisted that they were private.

Nell thinks back to the letter. The use of 'we' to suggest it was a communal invite. That the Iníons as a group were welcoming her to Rathglas.

– We all knew what we were getting into here, but you're not an Iníon – remember, you don't have to do everything you're asked.

Salt crusts at her hairline, forming a crystalline streak.

– Is that why you asked to meet down here?

– Partly. Every time I take a piss I wonder if she's in the next stall. I'm probably getting paranoid.

Nell can see a slight deflation in Muireann's way. Her sense of mischief dulled a little.

– Anyway – can I show you something?

She gestures for Nell to follow her. At one end of the cove, rising out of the water is a stone stake on a square plinth.

– Holy shit – is that the Levinson Stake?

– I thought you might be interested. Dates back a few centuries. Used to dispatch people accused of everything from treason and murder to sodomy and Satanism.

– I think I saw it from a distance as a kid out on the sea, but I've always wanted to see it up close. It looks weirdly smaller than I expected.

– But no less terrifying.

– How many people do you think they tied to it over the centuries?

– About a hundred, they reckon. Many of the early records were lost. The last case was a mother and her daughter accused of being witches in the 1850s. Locals said the daughter used to turn herself into a hare. And the mother turned the milk on every farm sour.

– And they tied them up and just left them?

– So much more satisfying for autocrats to watch supposed heathens drown slowly than burn fast, don't you think?

They stand in silence. Muireann looks resigned, shifting the equilibrium of the sack, back in practical mode. Nell thinks of Nick, who would no doubt love to hear this story later.

– Come on, you can help me shell the crabs up above.

38

When Nell arrives at Ryan's, he is sitting at a corner table, fiddling with a beer mat. His arrival on the island was a nine-day wonder, and the locals now just nod politely and don't bother him. Jimmy is propped up at the bar, regaling the fishermen. If he has seen her, he pretends not to.

Nell slides in beside Nick, their knees touching.

– I know it's a thing around here to say you're only 'going for one' – which I have discovered to mean 'several' – but tonight it can only BE one. Early work start.

– You should have said. We could have postponed.

– No, no, I wouldn't do that. Besides, I wanted to ask you about something.

He nods an order to Johnnie as if he's lived here all his life.

– About the Iníons …

– I've already told you. I really, really don't think you should approach them.

– You think it's a bad idea …

– They stay away from everyone and everything because they want to be left alone …

– But I promise I'd be respectful. I wouldn't intrude or get in the way. It just feels like ... someone should tell their story, in their words.

– I think Maman has that in hand.

– What exactly do you do out there?

Nell hesitates. Torn between wanting to hold his attention, impress him possibly, and loyalty to the women. And who would he even tell?

– I don't want to get into specifics.

– I'm a very good secret keeper, but I totally understand.

His face is earnest. Or it could be a face he produces at times to prove his trustworthiness. She could tell him, offer a crumb.

– They commissioned me to make something. As a way of preserving their history.

– Interesting ... why didn't they just do it themselves?

– I honestly don't know. I'm still trying to figure it out, but I guess it makes sense to ask an outsider, if you want a clear-eyed view.

– No baggage, no judgement.

– Exactly. Someone who will look at everything objectively.

– What are they like?

They don't know each other. The line of questioning feels too personal to Nell. It could be his American directness, or genuine curiosity, but there is something in it.

– You ask a lot of questions ...

He pinks slightly, composes himself.

- I'm sorry. I just want to learn as much about the island as I can.

- The island or the Iníons?

- I don't mean to overstep. OK, let's change the subject – do you enjoy working out there?

- Mostly. But it's another distraction. From my own work, you know? But I'm sort of into it now … so I have to see it through.

He absorbs all this while draining the end of a pint, foam clinging to his upper lip.

- See? I am living proof that you can actually have 'the one'? Unheard of in these parts.

He stands up and she laughs at this attempt at an island in-joke.

- Oh, you're actually serious?

- 'Fraid so. I have to tape an audition. My face needs to look hydrated, as if it got ten hours' sleep. Want a ride home?

On the drive back, he sings along with a song on the radio, off-key. It's oddly touching, this unguarded version of him. One hand on the wheel, the other on her thigh, the sea unseen, black against the night.

166

39

The heating at Rathglas is ancient and unpredictable. In the mornings, Nell works with her coat on. When the pipes eventually clang to life, the heating only highlights the staleness of the room. Lately she has been consumed by thoughts of a whole new life. Of starting over. It's not easy. If it was, everyone would be torching their farms or jobs or marriages and walking away without a backward glance.

A soft knock at the open door interrupts these thoughts. Maman stands, uncertain.

– Maman. Hi. Come on in.

The light in the studio makes the lines around her eyes more noticeable. It's hard to guess how old this woman is. A young sixty-five? Possibly an old fifty-five. Her movements are a little stiff, the ready dexterity of youth absent. A slowness in the bones, but still an air of authority.

– How's it all going?

– Getting there. The stories are tough, but they're important.

– I hope it's not too much for you?

– I leave the work here when I go home. Like a doctor or therapist. It's the only way.

Maman attempts a sympathetic look.

– Since you're making such good progress, I wondered if I might trouble you again. It's not my intention to overburden you, so I hope you won't mind what I'm about to ask.

A slump of Nell's heart.

– The book is of course very important to us, as you know, but there's something else I wanted to ask of you.

Nell pedals through the possibilities. Over Maman's shoulder, a sparrow lands on a tree. Paces the branch, shaking its head as if trying to dislodge something.

– I mentioned Samhain and our thirtieth anniversary, didn't I? And that I wanted to mark that. I owe thirty years of my life to these women and really want to do something memorable for them. So, I would be very much obliged if I could ask you to make something for it.

Push back, say no, Nell thinks.

Ignoring the lack of response, Maman pats the pockets of her smock, and retrieves a scrap of paper. A rough sketch of an object with some design suggestions.

– Now I'm not too fussed about materials, but let me know if you need anything, OK?

Nell focuses on the big globe sitting in its cradle, trying to figure out what to say.

– I'm not sure I …

She stops. Maman strives to hide her obvious disappointment and, sensing Nell's reluctance, moves to reassure her.

– Oh, it's quite an inconsequential thing – don't worry, it won't take long.

Afraid of saying the wrong thing, Nell chooses her words, speaking slowly.

– I hope you don't mind me saying this, Maman, but …
I thought I'd been commissioned just to work on the book.

It's brief, but unmissable. The ripple of tension across the older woman's shoulders. They stare at each other. Nell holds the gaze. The heater makes a tubercular gurgle and she is grateful for the interruption.

– Oh, of course. Where are my manners? Dear Nell. I'm impinging on your time in a ghastly way, when you've been so good to accept our invitation in the first place.

Nell doesn't want to let her down, or worse, have any conflict hovering over the project. She examines the drawing. It wouldn't take long to knock together. She has some fabric and other bits back at the cottage.

– I'm sure I could probably—

– No! Think no more about it. You've enough to be getting on with.

Maman picks up a folder from the desk and opens her mouth as if to speak. She changes her mind, silently returning it to the stack.

Nell knows there is only one answer, for everything to be OK.

– You know, it's actually no problem. I can make it.

Maman spins, face transformed and beaming.

– Oh Nell, I'm so grateful, thank you! I really want this year to be all about honouring Danu, our great protectress, and celebrating the world we've created here.

– It's fine. I'll make it work.

– Wonderful. I do appreciate that. Thank you.

She looks inordinately pleased with herself and moves to the door.

– *Suaimhneas*, Nell.

Nell pockets the paper, feeling slightly duped. She does not have endless time on her hands. She won't start the piece yet. Maybe she'll make Maman wait. Irked, her mind drifts to Cleary. Cathal says the boats will be arriving back later.

40

It's been two hours since the boat docked and Cleary is already on his fourth pint, veering close to whiskey chaser territory. It's a tradition, bailing to the pub as soon as the boat docks. The other lads will slag him off if he tries to get out of it. The day would have been better spent up the hills, hunting with Jimmy. He still feels bad about the hare. The glossy pelt. Her large, sad eyes.

The spell at sea was tough. Although Liam the skipper had insisted the weather would be fine, things got bad a couple of nights in. Waves throwing the boat around, the sea black and angry. Lying in the bunk, ashen, felt like circling a drain. A sort of grim Coriolis effect. The lads hadn't caught as much as they'd hoped. Liam said the catches just weren't the same as they used to be. He bragged that there used to be much more pollack out there. 'Shoals like whole islands. You could nearly stand on them.'

Some nights Cleary was too sick to make it to the toilet, instead vomiting over the side of the bed into an old catering tub of mayonnaise that Liam had discreetly deposited beside the bunk. Trying to block out the swirl in his gut, he thought of Nell. Quietly trying to get himself off when he was sure the others were asleep.

The whole thing between them had come out of nowhere. Returning from the mainland, he'd felt the lonely ache the island visits on people. The distance from everywhere else, the same faces, the tiny perimeter of land. The endless sea, rolling in, rolling out. He knew what some people said about her. But the heat, though. The fucking *heat* of it.

His own parents had been a disaster. Himself and the brothers carried the sadness of it. And the rage. It had left something deep in him, inked on the bones. It returned whenever there was a chance that something new might happen. It wasn't even fear. That would be easy to understand. It was worse than fear. Hope.

He threw an eye on the pub clock. Deciding whether to have one more. Which really meant three more, which meant messiness. Daytime gargling was brutal. Going to see her will not be an option if he has one more. The windows start to rattle. Surely a sign, or an answer.

– I'm away, lads. See yiz later. Get some kip, ye pricks.

He downs the last of his chaser and heads for the door. A hankering for a cigarette, so he wanders to the mini-mart to buy a pack. A gang of young Spanish women swarm outside the shop. Despite the beers, he's steady enough. Maybe the boat's helped his balance. He waits until he's across the forecourt and lights up. The smoke sour and delicious in his lungs.

There's a fork now. Decisions.

The lads in Ryan's. Or her cottage. Maybe he'll just give Jimmy a bell. Fuck knows, he's had enough of other people for a while. The smell of blokes. Never a minute to yourself on the boat. But the pub is right there. He pushes on the wooden door.

– There yiz are, lads. Miss me?

A large cheer goes up. One of the men begins an old song about a shipwreck and the ghost of a woman. Cleary raises his hand and orders another pint.

41

As Cleary is buying cigarettes, Nell is sitting in her car on
the road outside. She watches him chatting to Cathal, near
a stand of sun-bleached birthday cards. She doesn't want to
meet him here, not like this, and certainly not in front of
Cathal, who'd take it all in. Instead, she pulls out her phone,
types, deletes, retypes, one eye on the shop.

Heard you're back. Dinner at mine tonight – 8pm?

A group of women approach the shop, and Cleary holds
the door for them, pocketing a packet of smokes. Talking
loudly in Spanish, they giggle and pout. He looks good, but
tired. Thinner. The boats are hard. Anyone not used to
them can have trouble keeping food down. Nell watches
him retrieve the phone, read the text, and return it to his
jacket. His expression gives nothing away, but she's
impressed by whatever this mood is, caution or arrogance.

Instead of going home, she drives to the woods, flooring
the accelerator. She parks near a ditch, and the path is
muddier than usual, deep slick grooves making the going
hard. Barely a minute in and she has to move onto the verge,
nearer the trees. Already the sea is in sight, boiling away.
Fuck Cleary, ignoring her. And Maman, asking her for some-

thing. More work, more time. The rations bother her. Would there be war if she brought them food from her garden? It might make things worse. Seen as another intrusion.

Ferns sit low in the shade and the air teems with damp greenness. Like being underwater. It is possible to smell colour. To close your eyes and know that it reeks of a certain shade.

Halfway up, a sound. A few feet to the left. Branches stir, meeting resistance. The forest is all sound usually, but not like this. Nell stops, listening. Whatever caused it also stops. After a beat, she continues. A handful of steps and it's there again. To stop or keep going? She halts, tempted to call out. Don't. Do. A fox followed her home one night when she couldn't sleep and had gone for a walk. The whole time, it trailed ten feet behind, lingering until the cottage wall. Her breath is short, heart all amphetamine. Turning quickly, she feels certain that someone is standing among the trees in the distance, half hidden by a trunk.

– Hello?

The figure doesn't move.

Nell feels suddenly vulnerable. Her phone is in the car, and she curses herself for this lapse.

– Who's there?

There is no response. Just an indistinct shape in the branches. It does not move, but is, without doubt, watching her.

Her breath, quick now, mists the air. The light has turned and the day is starting to sink a little.

She runs through scenarios, trying to keep anxiety in check. The ground is too muddy to run, she'll get stuck, or fall.

Straining now, she can make out a figure of average height, but the shade of the trees offers little else.

Nell crouches, a pointless attempt to make herself less visible. When she looks up, the figure is gone. Without wasting a minute, she moves quickly down the path, trailing dread behind her until the car is in sight.

On the drive home, she leaves the radio off, shaken despite herself. She is working too much. Exhausted, edgy. Maybe there was nothing there at all. At the last bend in the road, the phone lights up on the passenger seat.

Not free tonight. Tomorrow at 8ish?

What could he be doing tonight? Maybe all that time at sea made him desperate, horny, and he's meeting with one of the Spanish gang. It's a petty thought, and she's annoyed for thinking it. He's more likely to be exhausted or catching up Jimmy. It feels like a game. Ignoring the text outside the mini-mart was a fuck-you. This message is curt and uneffusive, but still, it's not a 'no'.

It might feel strange to see him when all that happened before was intense. The new reserve is unnerving. If he'd stayed longer, there would have been more time to establish things.

There are no stars above the road tonight, a rare thing. No cloud cover, or rain forecast, but the sky is devoid of a single speck of starlight. There are omens everywhere if you look for them.

8 is good. See you then, sailor. Bring rum.

42

Nell's sleep was plagued by bad dreams. In one, it was the opening night of a show, and all the work had been hung incorrectly. None of the audio pieces had any sound and only one person showed up. In another, a large animal circled the house, and she spent the dream running to check the doors and windows.

A flask of coffee is almost empty but has helped move the morning in the studio along. She considers going to the kitchen to ask Sadhbh if she can make some more, but instead goes to find Muireann. Out beyond the animals, she is chopping wood. There is something in her movement that is not right. Breathless, and looking as though she might cry, but not from exertion. The emotion is unmistakably rage. Her shoulders rise upwards, knotted.

– Hey there, all good?

She swings the axe, splitting logs.

– Nope. Fucking Maman.

One hand is shaking and she takes a deep breath.

– What did she do?

Muireann aims a kick at the assembled pile of wood.

– Z stole a slice of bread from the kitchen. Maman found them eating it and HIT them. In the face.

– Jesus!

– Can you imagine? Actually slapped them. Z was completely humiliated.

– Where's Z now?

– Maman told them to go to their room, so I went to see if they were OK. I just don't know what the hell's going on here anymore.

– Take a breath, let's sit down.

– It wasn't just the slap – although that's bad enough. There was something else. Z said there was a kind of viciousness. Almost ... a sense of pleasure? That she had this look in her eye. Sort of satisfied. No, wait, *entitled*. That's the word they used.

– That's really messed up.

– I don't know – it's bad, right? I need to tell the others.

– What will you say to them?

– I don't know. Maman used to talk to me. To all of us.

– Maybe she's got stuff on her mind? Or is worn down having to look after all of you ...

– When I first arrived, we were so united. We had each other's backs. There was no obligation to tell people your story. Just do your fair share. Be considerate of everyone else ... I mean, that's still the same, but not Maman. She used to be more compassionate, and now ... she seems to want more from us. More restrictions, more rules, holding us all tighter to her. But none of this gives her the right to … there's never been violence at Rathglas.

Muireann's face is weary. An echo of some memory in it.

Nell sits on the trunk of a felled tree, chooses her next words carefully.

– I'm not for a moment going to defend violence, but maybe she just snapped because she's not OK. Is it worth asking her how she is?

– Maybe. But how she is or isn't feeling doesn't justify it.

Muireann wipes her face with the sleeve of her smock. Nell leans over and squeezes her arm, passes her a water bottle.

– Would it be helpful if I said something? As an outsider? She might talk to me without feeling like she was being ganged up on.

– I honestly don't know. I'll talk to Z and see what they think. But thank you, Nell, I do appreciate you offering to help. I better go.

Muireann walks back towards the house. Nell watches her go, the weight of it evident in her stoop. She could speak to Maman, but this might annoy the Iníons. On the other hand, the older woman might be glad of someone to talk to. Nell wonders what prompted the slap. How foolish.

She wraps a cloth around the axe, smooths down the handle and picks her way across the garden. The sea is hurling itself at the shore below, and the waves hiss like gravel being walked on.

By the time she returns, the stove in the studio has gone out and the room is gloomier. Muireann is probably telling the others now, an unenviable task. Nell retrieves her bike, exhaling the heaviness of the day, and pushes off into the fading light.

The cycle home is a struggle, muscles fizzing in protest. Urging her legs on, she pictures the cottage: the line of boots at the back door, mismatched cups hanging on hooks; the basket of random flotsam retrieved from the sea. Which makes her think of her own neglected work. In order to be productive— No, not productive, that's a word that belongs to factories and machinery. In order to *make work*, happiness is a contributor. *No, not happiness.* Maybe contentment. *No. Also not true.* She was wildly, deeply unhappy all through the banshee sound project, even though it's one of her most acclaimed pieces. No one could ever spot the misery that underpinned it. Maybe the trick is to keep moving. No dust can land, wheels don't rust. The danger of getting stuck. With the same life, person, role.

Same, same, same. That would be the worst thing that could happen.

She should have cancelled on Cleary. Legs pulse, tired muscles struggling over the hill.

At home, she flicks the switch to heat water for a bath. Lights the fire and boils a pot of water for pasta. She pours a large glass of wine and pulls the heavy sitting room curtains over to blot out the darkness. A small act to shut out the day, and all the strife at Rathglas. She worries for the women, especially Muireann.

She leaves the lights off and puts a match to a solitary candle. She plonks into the armchair by the fireplace and takes several glugs of wine. Her phone emits a low battery tone, and she cannot move from the chair to charge it. Pure weary. It takes an inordinate amount of time to struggle out of her jumper, knitted by a woman she met at a retreat. A Fair Isle pattern. Or one of those other isles not unlike this place. The wool is delicate and must be hand-washed. Her nose snags on the stale vinegar corner of armpit. The sweat of pedalling up and down those bad roads. When Cleary began calling over regularly, she smelled her skin beforehand, and again after he'd left; just to see if the encounter left a trace. An infusion. The fire is making her tired, and she closes her eyes for a moment. She wonders how the Iníons reacted when Muireann told them what happened to Z. She was caught between her feelings and her instinct not to get involved. She must check the pot, get the charger, finish the Iníons' book, make the other object for Maman, sort out her future …

But then there is a wail of beeping. She leaps awake from the chair towards the smoke coming from the kitchen and the burnt tang fills her mouth and nose. Grabs the brush handle in a stupor to bash against the smoke alarm. Throws the blackened, sizzling pot into the sink. *Cleary. Fuck.* Find phone, plug in charger. Fuck.

I'm outside.

Are you here?

Is everything OK?

Seven missed calls. What a time to conk out. But she has not been sleeping and her body insisted. It's too late to call now, and she doesn't want their first conversation in weeks to be a groggy apology, mumbled into the phone. She types *Sorry*, one-handed, which comes out as *Sordy*. *Fell asleep*, which sounds like an excuse, even though it's not. The bitter smell of burnt pot fills every room. She gropes her way to bed and crawls in, fully clothed.

43

The night is long, and despite a flatline of exhaustion, she wakes frequently. A feverish feeling, as though something is not right. As dawn etches the windows, she texts Cleary again. In the hours afterwards, looking at the blue rectangle in the dark, she wishes she hadn't. The day already feels too long. She will work at home. Eat properly, maybe go to the sea. Or she could take out a notebook, make plans, but this only heightens the pinpricks of dread. *Get up and work immediately.* Hockney painted that on a chest of drawers at the end of his bed. Clothes, boots, hat on and out to Banshla. Sea air has a way of filtering out the dread. If there's kelp, she could gather knots of it. Make a tincture for Muireann's anxiety.

Her dreams are full of finish lines never reached. Arriving home from Banshla, the door shut and cold air rising to meet her, she moves from room to room, searching. What is it she is meant to do? A lie-down to quieten her brain. The new work. Ideas often settle on the periphery: a place she can't quite reach, a blind spot. But she has to hope that it is there, working away, embedding itself into the subconscious.

For the longest time, it feels as though she has been waiting. For what, she is not sure, the desired object or mood unidentifiable.

Somewhere down the hill, a machine starts up. Chainsaw, angle grinder, something throwing gnarled decibels around. In her father's final days, like a child in the bed, someone was cutting or clearing or sanding with similar-sounding machinery. A background choir of metal screeching on stone. Every time she hears it now, it is a reminder of someone dying. Of waiting for death.

In the tree outside, a blackbird sits, oblivious to the noise. *Are you waiting too?*

Cleary takes his time responding. A handful of words, aloof, but agrees to come over later. In the garden that afternoon, she pulls vegetables for an elaborate meal. A peace offering. Too many side dishes, a glut of flavours. Although it's barely 8 a.m., she pulls cookery books off the shelves. Her mother's old Mason Cash mixing bowl. Pale blue, sleek. The good knife. A juicer. An armful of spices in jars, the ones she hasn't managed to grow. Fistfuls of wild garlic. She puts two fat bottles of white wine in the fridge. Takes the butter out to soften.

And there it is. The slight ring of static in the air. The sound *on the way.*

44

He arrives with a bottle of wine. The hint of a new beard, all scrub. A polite kiss on the cheek. No entangled march to the couch, no urgency. A note of distance. Her hands reek of garlic. The clothes she never got around to changing are smudged with sauce and a dusting of flour.

It is important to make an effort with the dishes. To make a fuss. He ignores the chestnut soup. Tries not to gag when the roast fennel hits the back of his throat.

– I thought you'd be starved after all the time on the boat. Fish every day for dinner?

– Not really. There's a cook.

– You not hungry?

– No ... no, I am ... I just. I'm happy with a pork chop. A simple man, me. Steak, burgers, a chicken in the oven on Sundays.

– Is it a bit much? Sorry.

– Nah, it's grand. Thanks for making it anyway.

– Tell me – how was the boat?

– Bumpy, endless. The fucking smell. Fish, sweaty blokes, diesel. Awful.

He is quiet again. What must it have been like, spending all that time out there.

Between bites and sips, he binds his lips together. It's a disconcerting act, as though trying to keep the food down, politely masticating. Neither finishes their food, and they move to the bedroom. It is usually his habit to hold her afterwards, whispering thoughts into the gaps of her verte-brae. A kind of a ritual, praying to her spine. Tonight, he nods off quickly, his feet running in the sheets before moving into a deep trench of sleep. Limbs twitching, eyes rolling under his lids.

Nell lies awake. The emptiness of the night weighs heav-ily. The end of a situation is its own funeral. She contemplates getting up to make mint tea.

And then it starts.

As a tap, low but insistent. A familiar rhythm. The *roll-ing, rolling, rolling* of notes. All that can be done is to wait for it to pass and hope that the impact will be minimal. See what aftermath will follow.

In the dark, the room is gripped by each rising note. Once, it fascinated her. But now, each year, it feels incre-mentally more sinister.

Cleary wakes, bleary, unsure of his surroundings. The light from the bathroom echoes yellow, and when he turns to face her, his eyes are black, not green. They widen, his panic evident.

– Fuck!

– It's OK, don't worry.

– What the fuck …

It takes her a minute to figure out what's happening.

– You can hear it, can't you?

Bathed in citrus light, the realisation sinking in, Cleary's face transforms. He leaps from the bed, grabbing his clothes.

– You did this! It's you!

The air fills with static. Nell tries to speak. The sound rumbles around the room.

– I've lived on this fucking island my whole damned life and I've NEVER heard it! Not once! Not when my whole family could, and I thought I was the one losing my mind.

The veins on his neck bulge. His agitation makes her nervous. There is no way she can persuade him back to bed. He hops, battling a trouser leg, shouting.

– I don't want this.

– It's OK – it'll stop soon. I know yo—

– It drove my father mad, Nell. Do you have any idea?

– Please, please calm down. Come to me.

– He went batshit crazy.

– There's nothing to be afraid of. Please trust me.

Nothing Nell says diffuses the situation. Even she is unconvinced by her own words. Cleary dresses in a frenzy.

– And why now, huh?

– I don't understand why now. Please! Just sit down until it passes.

The sound whirls on. Cleary is sweating, spittle-lipped.

– After all these years. Not a single peep – and you know what? I was GLAD.

He jabs a triumphant finger in her face.

– I'll fucking tell you *why now* …

The shoes he kicked off earlier trip him, causing more fury. Nell puts a hand on his to offer comfort, but he yanks it away.

Everything has changed. His face close to hers, eyes stretched in panic.

– This is YOU.

– What are you on about? Cleary! Please, you're being ridiculous.

– *You're* ridiculous, do you know that? You're a fucking joke. They all talk about you in the town.

A pause, his body beyond agitated.

– And Jimmy warned me about you.

– Jimmy?

She cannot think about what Jimmy might have said. What poison he's poured in his nephew's ear. Cleary ignores her.

– What was in the food? Hmm?

– The food?

– The goddamn herbs. Your weird medicine. Christ, MY EARS.

He snatches his coat from the floor, knocking over a wine glass. He is out the door before she can find something to cover herself with. She is cold and feels faint.

But she must go after him. Chasing the squelch of tyres on mud, the car bouncing down the track. Nell finds herself naked under the moon, vulnerable. Afraid in a way

189

that she rarely feels. She thinks suddenly of the figure in the woods.

The hum throbs on, frequency bursting across the hills.

Through the open car window, Cleary bellows into the night.

– *Wiiii-ttch! You fucking witch!*

At the end of the track, the car squeals right and he is gone, taillights fading into dark. The whole world of them has turned upside-down. Whatever they'd had left, capsized. Icy waters. Lifeboats. Something sharp presses into her heel, a tiny wound spreading. Aware of her body exposed to the air. The chill suits this cruel ending. There is nothing else to do. All that remains is the sound pulsing, a pace as frantic as her heart, turning the same beat over and over.

PART THREE

45

Nell wakes to quiet. The room is cold, grey light in pockets on the floor. There is no option to stay in bed, even though that's what she most desires. She showers, dresses quickly, with extra layers for the studio and the day's work ahead. It's the last thing she feels like doing, especially with Maman's additional request. It's not fully bright. The lights for the bike are nowhere to be found. Daylight won't be long.

On the bike, she pedals furiously, replaying Cleary's shouts. The fraught image of him speeding away into the night. The morning is one of those dull, bleak affairs. It presses on her and she tries to focus on the sea as it dips and disappears along the route. At Rathglas she dismounts, and notices Z heading up the driveway.

– Where are you off to?

Z stops briefly, but then seems to think better of it.

The gravel crunches as they stomp down the drive. On their shoulder, Z carries a tote of the same coarse material as the Iníons' smocks. They are wearing an old pair of baggy suit trousers and a too-big jacket. The youngest of the Iníons, they look haggard, older.

– Wait! Hey!

Z picks up the pace, determined not to stop. It makes her uneasy, but all Nell can do is watch them pass through the gates. She turns to push her bike the rest of the way and knows she is being watched.

After the scene on the driveway, the halls are strangely silent. Muireann is nowhere to be found. She wants to talk about last night. Have someone comfort her. It has caught her off guard, how much she looks forward to their talks. Muireann possesses a self-containedness Nell admires. Perhaps for too long, Nell has been on her own. Too self-reliant. Solitude can be its own kind of loss. It's a pity Muireann is in this place and not out in the world. She imagines them meeting for swims, picnics on the beach in summer.

But Muireann has opted for another life, just as Nell chose hers. That is the way of the world, of people. The intersections and near misses, the fact that we all make our own choices.

In the kitchen, some Iníons are boiling fleeces for lanolin. Nell looks in on the weed shed and the chapel. In the cliff garden, Ebele is hanging wool on a clothes line to dry. They ignore her or are too immersed in the slow ritual of it, full of care. Nothing suggests that anyone is aware of Z's departure. The wind blows the pelts softly, and Nell thinks of canvases waiting to be stretched and painted. When she asks them if they've seen Muireann, Ebele reveals that she is ill and resting. Maman has given instructions for her not to be disturbed.

The benches in the garden are deserted. It's unusual to see so few Iníons outside in the morning. Inside, Nell passes the dining room and Aurora is being comforted by Rose. Aisling looks ashen. By the studio, Sile is mopping the corridor floor and before Nell can ask what has happened, Sile jerks her head towards the studio. Nell quickly opens the door and as soon as they're inside, words spill out.

– Oh Nell, I'm so glad to see you. Everything has gone mad. I've never seen Rathglas this divided.

There are deep shadows under her eyes, and a feverishness to her manner.

– I know Mother Maman says Muireann is ill, but she's not.

– What's the matter then?

– She's devastated about Z leaving.

– I just saw them on the driveway – what happened?

– They're gone for good. Over the other thing.

– Being hit?

Sile stares at the ground, a flashback of shame on her face.

– Muireann is furious. It's not like her to take to her room but she's so angry with Maman. Rose is afraid she'll do something.

Despite Rathglas's proclaimed democratic tenets, like most groups, there would always be factions, sides, politics. Nell knows she should go and check on Muireann. Z deserved better. But after last night with Cleary, she cannot bear any more drama.

– This is the first time anyone has ever left, Nell. It's never happened.

– I don't know what to say. But feel I should try to stay out of it – but I promise I'll talk to Muireann, OK?

Poor Z. Maybe she should go after them on the bike, offer to put them up for a couple of nights, until they figure out a plan. But she knows she must not get involved.

– It's a real shame that it's come to this. I'll really miss them. We all will.

When Sile is gone, Nell tries to work, to bury herself in the project. Pushing thoughts of Cleary – his sour words, the curdling of the whole thing – out of her head. A gull lands on the ledge outside, too big, its wings tapping the window.

46

On the way home, drained and anxious, she takes a different route across the fields. Moving through the green wall of it, blades slapping the spokes. After dinner, tormented by retracing her argument with Cleary again and again, she makes a nightcap to help her sleep. Her lids have barely closed when a sound pierces the quiet. Nell wakes to the phone ringing, trying to gauge its location. Following the shrill ring, a sudden reminder of an inventory: the many phone calls of her life alone. Test results, cold calls about electricity, bank managers, bad news. The gossipy ones that can't be written down. Or the good calls. Ones you want to last for all time. Urgent confessions. Erotic. Words whispered only to someone trusted. As though they happened to someone else in another life. Voices ventriloquised, hushed exchanges, her mouth a conduit.

There was a time, not too long ago, when there was only one phone on the island. Hanging like a votive on the wall of Ryan's. Such scarcity meant a hierarchy of access. The doctor, the vet and Paddy who runs the ferry orbited around it, messages taken and delivered.

Hello?

No, no, no, yeah, no, no. Sure.

I'll seeya, bye, bye, bubye bubye.

Countless words spoken into the greasy mouthpiece.

I love you.

Come quickly.

No can do.

Glaciers between the gaps, the things unsaid. Withholding.

Nell moves from room to room in the cottage, tracking the ringing to the kitchen table; the screen reads *Cleary*. Patience. Understanding. This is what she should offer. She'd never seen him rattled, agitated. Maybe this is who he really is. Like so many other men she has encountered, who felt entitled to her.

No, that's unfair. *The sound. The fucking sound.*

She remembers the first time her father heard it. Locked himself in the bathroom with a bottle of whiskey until it was over.

Cleary must have felt let down but the thing between them had no borders drawn, no definitions. The way she likes it. In truth, they barely know each other, so how can she possibly gauge his hurt, his fear? And now that was probably it. Over before it had a chance to really start. Last night was severed in two: his life before and after hearing the sound. The fear was understandable. The poison of it, working its way in, towards anvil, hammer, stirrup.

What to say? What to offer?

The phone rings out on the table.

47

Maman returns the ledger to the drawer and lets out a long, weary breath. After the last few days, a conversation with Muireann is needed but she cannot bear it. Having to stand there and ask for mercy all because someone has left? There is nothing she can say to justify the slap. Although, no one likes a thief. Even if she brought out the ledger and waved the columns around, all the calculations she does to make sure Rathglas will be here next month, next year. They must find a way to persist. It isn't looking good. The weather has been too unpredictable, affecting what they can grow. Her smock feels heavy, stultifying, hair sweating under a head-scarf. Opening the window makes little difference and she feels it then, the familiar dread, the suffocating anticipation. As though trees might fall, or the moon might fail to rise.

She will command the novices to put a candle in every window. The Iníons must plan. For the future, for survival.

The air is leaden, and she knows the familiar notes of the sound are waiting, birds on a wire. It might be two hours, or four, but the sound is gathering itself, and the night will not be undisturbed by it.

* * *

That night the Iníons gather in the hall and sing until dawn. Muireann stays in her room. Maman is nowhere to be seen. Each note heaves the sun higher and higher, dispelling the dark.

An offering.

48

Cleary's voicemail is almost neutral. Like someone reading through a checklist. An apology for the name-calling, an explanation promised for his behaviour. A line about needing to get away. From everything. The island. The sound. Maybe that means it isn't her he's running from. Either way, he's gone. The job on the rigs came through, and it was a good enough reason to leave. Out of the bay, into the deep indigo, to the noise and spires of the drill rigs. Fear in his voice, a slight muffle. Maybe he had a few drinks before he called. Or took a pill.

Nell feels an absence of how she thought she would. Before the distance grew. She had felt it in herself, a hardening, but this could be an old trick. Self-protection. Christ, she wants no more of this. Wading out too far. Even a single step beyond and the whole shelf slips out from beneath you, down into the cold, feet pedalling in panic, digging to find the floor. Nell can't bear that feeling. She wants to make the lighthouse piece. Maybe she'll perform it for longer than a week. Reacquaint herself with being alone. A durational act of solitude.

49

There were no albatrosses, no ominous clouds this time. Just a marrow-deep unease among those attuned to it. The sun had been out most of the week, a saffron haze warming the rocks. An unseasonal temperature that might have been a sign in itself that the sound was on its way. The fishermen had been uncharacteristically jokey, ribbing each other as they swabbed the decks, glad of the light and the good weather. Afterwards, some commented on the calendrical vantage of it; that it started on a Sunday, the first day of the week for some, the day of worship for others.

When the sound finally stopped, the people on the island who could hear it experienced mass tinnitus that lasted hours. Some were awake all night, fearful, counting the hours until daylight. People were banging down Dr Foran's door long before the surgery was open.

On the dot of noon the next day, their hearing returned, like an unexpected shout. Some reported blood spots on their collars and jawlines.

A newspaper attempted to link it to climate phenomena. Levied that it was a claxon of environmental doom. The story predicted which mainland cities and towns would be under water in the next twenty-five years. The capital, certainly. Anywhere within 20 kilometres of the coast. The island would be hit hard, the town and most houses across the lowlands and coves would be submerged. All except for Rathglas, clinging to its isolated cliff 300 metres above the sea, the highest point on the island, looking out towards Danu.

Nell was in the studio the next day and desperately wanted to know how Rathglas was affected. No one stopped by, so she couldn't ask. Today, there was no delivery of a pot of tea. Everyone appeared to be still brooding on Z's departure and Nell sensed a palpable splintering. Muireann had hardened towards Maman, to the routines of the day, even to some of the other Iníons. Samhain couldn't come soon enough. The dark nights were drawing in, and she longed to be away back home.

50

Far out on the rig, the men have been drinking. Someone fell into the sea yesterday and, if not for the survival suit, a red beacon bobbing out on brutal waves, he'd have been lost. The lads are still a bit shook. An exception was made when someone brought out a bottle of whiskey. Another man returned from his cabin and sheepishly contributed two naggins of rum. It broke the ice. The hard lid they kept on their lives. Talk of kids and missing the football, walks up mountains.

Cleary has been there just over a week. The only one who hails from the island. Someone asks about the sound. Tongue thickened with booze, inarticulate, he feigns ignorance. Doesn't mention he's recently become acquainted with the drum and pulse of it. He tries to ignore the swells of nerves in his chest. It's heading for midnight, so he mumbles an excuse, bids them all goodnight. A decent bunch. Irish, Scottish, Norwegian. Places of rain and long winter days.

The cabins are hot and stuffy. It's never quiet. Machinery rattling, men coming and going to shifts. Most nights a pill helps. A bad idea with the booze, but it might guarantee a decent first sleep of his stay.

He listens to music, watches a show on YouTube about killer whales, and waits for the drugs to hit. Miles from here, Nell is probably in bed. Swiftly, there are scenarios, images in his mind, he picks up the phone. *Don't do it, man.*

He types *hello*. Deletes. Tries again, different tone. Backspaces. Throws down phone. Opens porn on the laptop. Picks up the phone again. Leaves a long voice message. Maybe she will understand. He lies down, mind whirring, imagining the lights of the harbour. A cold pint in Ryan's. What happened after the sound. Her face. Her face. Only her face.

51

Whales were part of the island life. Minke, Fin. Humpback. Boats brought tourists out in droves, depending on the weather. Occasionally one would wash up, bloated and discoloured. The last one was a sperm whale, *Physeter macrocephalus*. Cachalot. A baleful Leviathan.

But that whale had nothing on the one that washed up at Dodder Bay. A sperm whale, a giant beast. It was pitiful to see it stilled and lifeless. A marine biologist from the institute on the mainland was dispatched on the first ferry. In her view, the creature was not long dead, but something had already had a go at it, judging from the bites gauged into its heft. The large portion of ambergris in its belly caused a scramble. Nell had wanted it, even a sliver, for Muireann, but two fishermen got into a fistfight over the spoils. She overheard Paddy and Cathal saying that no good would come of it showing up.

Nell tells Muireann about the whale to distract from the tension between her and Maman. She leaves Rathglas early that day, heading across to Dodder Bay with her camera. The creature's belly gleams like grey glass. Muscles, once taut, all torsion, flop to one side of a large wound. It is almost vulvic, gleaming. In a few days the smell will be rank. Gas trapped in its gut escaping, through the long process of decomposition or birds pecking holes in the corpse. She moves around, snapping from different angles. She might send them to Cleary. Some island news to keep the line open. Nothing more non-committal than being sent an image of a dead whale.

Later, when she sends them, he jokes that they're not the kind of images he was hoping for. She could send something now. A curve of breast, a flash of underwear. Flicking back through all the whale images, there is one, zoomed in on its guts. So close that even looking at it now on her bed, far from the beach, makes her retch a little. She sends it, along with an accidental shot of her feet from earlier.

52

It is difficult to slough off other people's worries. To scoop out the sediment that has settled in your own bones. She thinks of Cleary's broken family. His father losing his mind at the sound. No wonder he panicked and ran into the night. She is relieved not to hear from Nick. One less thing to worry about.

She has just finished a book about the wife of a famous painter. The woman used to contact galleries on his behalf, answer correspondence, keep record of his output. She was also his subject, appearing in many of the paintings, not just as herself, but as an archetype of the wife. A lone woman, in a hotel room, on the street. The wife was also a painter but was not as well-known as the husband. They fought, it was said, with much violence. He wanted her to prioritise housework over art, to paint less. Gradually she gave in to his pressure and called her own paintings by terrible names. She recognised that there was only room for one of them to succeed.

When she turns off the light after being immersed in their turbulent life, Nell feels furious. Depressed even. She has always known – and been comforted by the fact – that

she is not *wife material*. A group of the lads said as much,
chortling over their pints in the smoking section out the
back of Ryan's. Nell was in the ladies, a solitary dank cubi-
cle with an avocado toilet bowl. Mid-piss, she'd listened
impassively through the open window as they discussed
several island women and the merits and faults of their
breasts. One of them brought up her name, but before there
was time for an appraisal, he made the wife comment.
Unmarriable. *Thank fuck for that*, she thought.

It's better to inspire fear than pity; desire not scorn. She
flushed, reapplied her lipstick and walked back into the bar,
defiant, amused.

In her early work, Nell had certainly been more fearless.
It made sense to not care what an audience might say. A few
summers back, she created an installation in different loca-
tions on the island, about embodiment and voice, pivoting
around ideas of speaking up, voicelessness, silences. At a
time when she used a lot of sound and audio, experimenting
with pitch and frequency. The main section of the piece was
located in the forest. Sculptures of women from the island's
history. Roisin Rua, a shawl-maker, Danu. Each contained
a motion-sensitive speaker that triggered a voice when
someone walked past it. Down at the cliffs near the beach,
speakers hung from large poles in the sand held in place
with metal cables. They broadcasted a siren song on a loop
as if attempting to lure sailors. Every night she went to the
beach to hear it, comforted by the high notes, taking solace
in her ability to bring something into being. Not everyone

liked it. Some found it unsettling. A petition of complaints was submitted to the mainland council, and it was removed after just ten days.

On an island that grapples with a recurrent hum phenomenon, the eerie sound work was probably a misstep. An unwelcome reminder of the uncanny notes that plague this place.

In another life, she could be someone else's wife. Or a botanist, or trapeze artist. Swinging on a meniscus rope every night. She might even be what Cleary said, a witch. *Wife. Mother.* Those words are of no interest. *Artist.* That is the only thing that matters. *Iníon.* Did Maman decide that's what they should be called?

If it was possible to stop time, she would. To make all the things she wants to make. It feels, some days, that the things that matter are slipping away. Two opposing kinds of momentum. The urge to resist involvement. With men, jobs, collaboration. To keep to herself. That's what has always worked. The simple throughline, its disconnection, is its own kind of freedom.

She eats dinner by the fire, restless, feeling each morsel lodge in her chest. Washing it down with a third glass of wine, Nell studies the stripped fish bones on her plate. A creature that never contemplated its own fate, never thought for a moment about its oval frame, the translucent skeleton. A shape more sophisticated than a human's cuspate angles. Our heavy knee bones, all cauliflowered at the joint; the clunky, bitty phalanges.

Life drawing was her favourite class at college. The lines and angles, the sheer reality of flesh and fat and muscle. Strangers allowing you to look at them for hours. The attempts to capture their bodies on the page while knowing nothing about who they were after leaving the room. She'd like to draw the Iníons for the book, but maybe she should have done that earlier. When they had not known each other. But that too could be considered an overstep. A breach of the tentative trust they've formed. And without knowing why, for sure, Maman would likely not have allowed it.

She drains the glass, spring florals blooming in her mouth.

53

A team from the mainland has arrived to deal with the whale. The stench has stalked the town for days now. Seeping under door cracks, in through heating vents. Anyone foolish enough to leave a window open soon regretted it. Given the creature's size and slow deterioration of its flesh, detonation was considered the best option. There aren't many houses near this spot. The dynamite charges were set against the outside of the whale's body to blow it towards the sea. A buffet for the creatures in the bay, the passing gulls.

On the day of detonation, a curious crowd gathered at a distance. People sat in groups in the dunes, passing around foil-wrapped sandwiches and flasks of tea. Davey Lawlor drove his four by four on to the beach, hoping to pick up some bits for bait. There was great excitement when the countdown started, but when the charges went off, things didn't go as planned. Only half the carcass exploded, and mostly not in the direction of the sea. Bits of whale viscera rained down on the spectators. A large piece of bone dented the roof of Davey's car, smashing the windscreen.

It took several more days to get rid of it. Teams working round the clock on the decimated corpse, cutting it into chunks. People joked about the island gulls being too heavy to get airborne afterwards, their guts engorged with whale meat for days.

54

The days are getting shorter, and Nell turns the studio lamps on early to keep writing. The Iníons' stories are enlightening, often grim. Each trying to live an existence centred on meaning, substance. Reading them has created in Nell a strong ache to get back to the cottage. To the carrion of her work. The book belongs to the women of Rathglas, it's for them, but the process still cleaves closely to the familiar arc of her practice. She'd forgotten it. The point in the genesis of every project that feels like walking a high wire between two buildings. Too far across to turn back, gritted teeth to get to the other side. It's happened nearly every time: the banshee audio, the Japanese speakers. The conflicted possibility of what to do or make. Inching closer to the other end of the wire. At least the book felt like a legacy. One that wasn't being made at the expense of her spirals, or the Greenawn burial project. Oh, to be at Banshla now. All seafoam and shoreline. Blue caves, black rocks.

Many islanders swim year-round at Banshla, Greenawn, a couple of the smaller sheltered coves. It's not for the faint-hearted. It's only October but the water already feels glacial. The urgent shock of it. The pull of the sea is hard to shake. Wading into the waves is a chance to step off the island for a while. Last summer there was a rogue patch of phosphorescence at Cloughkeel beach, a psychedelic wreath. Tonight, in the dark swell there is only the sound of a lone whale, and Danu above. How lonely to be always reaching out for someone who isn't there.

I'm here.

Tell me,

I'm listening ...

Nell thinks of her grandmother, her hands clutching Nell's as they paddled on this same beach. Her hard life of labour and scarcity. Her shattered body, trapped in a constant cycle of birthing, carrying, washing. Desire out of her reach. Untouched except in acts of wifely duty. Maybe it's presumptuous to assume this. Her and Grandfather might have craved each other. Stolen occasional afternoons in bed, the children sent to the far field to pick apples. Sun streeling in over breast and hip, dappled and loved. Both gone now, buried in the graveyard on the cliff. Marking spirals on the shore is an acknowledgement of impermanence. That the shoreline will be gone someday, the island too. But the sea will survive and whenever there is sand, then everything settles in the end. The island is part of her, part of what she tries to make. Deep down, she suspects this is why she has never left. Nor did her grandmother, superstitious about leaving the island's blue haze behind on the horizon.

Cleary never spoke of his grandparents. Or his parents, except for the night of the sound. Only Jimmy. Their bond seems genuinely tender, not predicated on obligation, and yet it was Cleary who came back to the island because there was no one else to look after Jimmy. Of all the things she had observed about him since that first day on the beach, she had overlooked kindness. She treads water, the cold stinging now, and looks around wondering in which direction the rig is. Good money, but tough, mind-numbing work. Not much craic to be had with the kind of lads who sign up. Big-armed burly guys who could winch a man up single-handedly if he fell off the platform. Men you wouldn't spend a minute with if you weren't all locked up together at sea. Nell pictures him, lying in his low bunk counting the hours until his shift. Thinking of Jimmy, or her. What he might do after the rig and the boats.

At home, she warms her legs at the fire. Mottled purple, still sluggish from the cold. She types out a message. *Are you awake?*

No reply. Her message, delivered, unread.

Before bed, she smokes in the kitchen, out the window. She never likes to stand with the back door open, despite the safety of the island. Too much darkness for the lights of the house to counter. A fox screams beyond the garden. As familiar as it is, the cottage sometimes feels too isolated. The figure in the woods still causes unnerving thoughts. The moon climbs up, a chunk bitten out of its side. Familiar stars are draped around, and she picks them out while tipping ash into the night. When she finally falls into bed, the sheets clean and cold, she snaps an image from the waist up and sends it before turning off her phone. She sleeps as though returned from war.

55

The next morning, the driveway to Rathglas is flanked by yellow spears of Mahonia. The last flags of colour before the low light and monochrome of the building. Buddleia – a nemesis she'd struggled to banish from her own garden – runs amok on the perimeter wall. Aisling, wearing a heavy coat, is doing battle with a blunt-looking pair of shears. Nell switches on her phone.

– Good morning, Nell. Maman asked to see you – she's in the cliff garden.

To deter any further enquiry, Aisling promptly returns to slashing at the messy scribble of stems before her.

Nell's phone pings.

Appreciate the photo. Wish I was there.

Sent at the end of his shift last night, it feels more intimate, incongruous to read it in daylight, especially at Rathglas. On the nights he is most lonely, he dispenses with words, sending voice notes instead. The background is always filled with clanking sounds, the dull mechanics of the rig. If he's in his cabin, he whispers over the loud gurgle of his bunk mate's snores.

* * *

Around back, Maman sits at the table, eyelids closed, sheer and oily. Reminiscent of petals. The headscarf is drawn tightly under the chin, her robe neat and minimal. A clear winter sun is up, shimmering on the rocks. The trees are skeletal, carpets of leaves ringed beneath them. The wind carries the stench of the compost heap, but Maman seems unperturbed by it.

– My dear Nell. Sit, sit.

Her arms are crossed. A gesture that could be construed as matronly or guarded.

– There's bad weather on the way. I can feel it. Maman adjusts her headscarf as if to guard against it.

– I've lived here all my life and have long given up trying to predict the weather, other than an obvious guess at a chance of wind and rain.

– I'm a bit of a weathervane, actually. Some people feel it in their bones – you know, the ones who give out about their rheumatism? For me, it's more of a tang in the mouth, a sort of phantom taste as if I'd just eaten something when I haven't.

– I get that about the sound.

– You do?

– Yes, sometimes. A feeling on my skin. Not quite an itch, or tingle. Somewhere in between. Never get any advance warning about the weather though. But I do like when the wind is up. You know those really full-on gales? If you're inside, of course. Feeling safe.

– Do you feel safe here?

– At Rathglas?

– On the island.

– Of course. I know this place like the lines on my own palm.

Nell doesn't mention smoking out the kitchen window at night. Maman sweeps a stray leaf off the table and looks towards the chapel.

– I know I'm not a local, but I really do feel the same. Especially about our little corner of the island.

Nell waits for Maman to get to the point, but it's an opportunity too. She waits a minute, thinks about not saying anything but ignores the hesitation.

– I'm glad you asked to see me, actually. Muireann came to the studio this week and we got talking.

– Oh yes?

A slight stiffening. She holds Nell's gaze.

Nell wants the conversation to be over and is immediately alert to the fact that this invoking Muireann's name may cause problems for one or both of them.

– She … Well … I don't know if it's my place—

– If you think it isn't your place then it probably isn't.

Maman smiles from the eyes down. Nell wants to both hold her ground and retreat. The wind gathers pace, and Nell wishes she'd worn another layer.

– OK, then can I ask another question – about the archives?

– Fire away.

– I'm working my way through them, right, and there are folders for everyone here, women who've died, all the early residents. But, as far as I can see, there's nothing for you ...

– No.

– So you didn't provide a testimony.

– I chose not to.

– But why is that, when you say everyone else had to?

– No one *had to*, Nell, they were invited in the spirit of community and healing, and they chose to tell their stories.

– OK then, why didn't you choose to tell yours?

Maman sighs and then takes a staggered breath. For the briefest moment, Nell sees the face she saw in their first meeting. Open, unconflicted.

– I ... just didn't know where to start.

Nell had expected haughtiness, even irritation, but not this. It's oddly vulnerable. As real as she's seen Maman be. She tries to think of the right thing to say. A word that might offer encouragement.

– Not everything that happens to us is a story. And certainly not one we have to tell to others.

The older woman looks anguished at sharing even this small admission. All at once, it's clear that this is someone used to dealing with their own problems, figuring things out. It is, Nell senses, difficult for her to balance this conflict. Running Rathglas must require a distance, a need to hold personal emotions in check. The last person she'd want to reveal anything to is an outsider. They sit without speaking for a while. Nell wants her to talk – to feel – that she can talk. Maman uncrosses her arms and pulls the chair closer.

– If we could get back to the reason I wanted to see you … I'd like to ask – and only if you want to – if you'd like to join us for the Samhain ceremony? To celebrate with us. As a thank-you for all your hard work.

– I do appreciate the offer, thank you. Now that I'm nearly finished, I've my own work to get back to, but I'll see how I go.

– Well, the offer is there. And there's a spare room in the attic too, if you want to stay over with us.

– Can I let you know?

Maman tilts her head, her eyes flinty, a curious smile forming.

– You don't like me, Nell, do you?

Nell is taken aback by her directness, even more than the earlier vulnerability. Maybe that had been a ploy, an attempt to draw her in. It's hard to know. She's been coming here for weeks and Maman is still so opaque.

– I … this is a working relationship for me, Maman. I've always found you to be nothing but cordial and fair, regardless of what else is going on here …

– 'What else is going on here' – whatever that implies … Things can get blown completely out of proportion.

– I hardly thin—

– Do you think we'd have survived all this time if someone wasn't prepared to make the hard decisions? To think beyond themselves? And as you said yourself earlier, Nell – it is not your place. I didn't ask for much, but I asked you to respect our privacy. So, thank you for your time and your work. I'll let you get back to it.

Maman sweeps across the grass, her smock uneven, the back hem skimming her ankles. Nell follows her long shadow moving back towards the house. Her voice was full of emotion, and the words seemed genuine, but it is hard not to feel a little stung by the chastisement. She feels the drop in temperature acutely; only a couple of degrees, but enough to encourage her to go back inside. Passing the hedge, Nell notices Sile, who has been listening the whole time, walk briskly away.

Last week, Nell overheard Aurora telling one of the more recent arrivals about the ceremony held every year on 1 November. Because no individual birthdays were marked at Rathglas, Samhain was treated like a communal celebration. Of course it had religious connotations, but there was a sense of dispensing with some routines. The one day of the year to slough off formalities.

Maybe she'd stay over. See if the ceremony revealed any more about these women who, after all these weeks, still remained a mystery.

Her phone lights up. A text from Nick.

I need to speak to you. Drink in Ryan's tomorrow night at 7?

56

The day ends with heavy rain, and a sky of metal shades. The corridor is busy, with Iníons in and out of the room at the end of the hall. The shock at hearing a big ripple of laugher, after how strained everything has seemed to be around here. The meeting with Maman hadn't ended the way she wanted. It felt like a test. She has no change of clothes – her jumper is speckled with paint and smelling of turps but it will have to do for Ryan's. When she arrives, the usual coterie of drinkers is there. Billy and some lads from the boats are quietly supping at the bar. Nick is already there and immediately something is off. A sway, the weighing-scale slump of his shoulders.

– HEEEYyyyyy!

It takes her a moment to realise that he's extremely drunk. Several cream-ringed pint glasses are lined up on the ledge beside him.

– Well, how-DEE-do. How are you, mizz?

A fake bow, mock etiquette. The vaguely antebellum nature of it is weird. This southern drawl resurfaces when he's drunk, the accent greased by booze. Nell raises an eyebrow half-jokingly to indicate displeasure at whatever it is he's doing. She has always had a soft spot for jolly, messy drunks. Spilling over with confessions, and so pliable. Likely to be talked into things.

At a guess, the listing roll in his stance suggests four, maybe five pints. A flake of toilet paper clings to the toe of his expensive trainers, the leather a just-out-of-the-box shade of unmarked white.

– Is this your boho artist look?

He waves a hand towards the jumper, spilling the head off a pint.

– Coming from work and no time to change.

She eases herself onto a high stool and nods an order to Johnnie.

The actor's eyes widen, and he leans in all clumsy, whispering.

– Ooo. With the Iníonsssss …

The hiss is deliberate. A pleasure in it.

Nell ignores this. He straightens up.

– Sorry, sorry sorry, Nelly.

– It's Nell.

Hovering by her ear now, he leans on the snug door, which wobbles on its hinges.

– I'm a lil' soused.

– Bit early to be so soused? I don't think there's enough hours for me to catch up.

– Weellll, I'm celebrating, you see? And I want to thank you for your help. I nearly talked this here gentleman

Johnnie into selling me a bottle of champagne, but there's none to be had in this noble establishment.

He pulls her closer in a clumsy hug, reeking of stout. Johnnie, drying glasses with a tea towel, keeps an eye on the situation.

– Help with what?

– Hell, I couldn't have done it without yoooou. Thank you! Woooo!

He punches the air and stumbles forward. Before she can catch him, he hits the ground. Johnnie is out from behind the bar like a light.

– You're all right, son, you're all right.

Nick allows himself to be pulled up, Nell realising the weight of him.

– Listen, he's had a skinful, love, maybe he'd be better off at home. You parked outside?

Nodding, she follows Johnnie out the door, his arm around the actor's back, half walking, half dragging him to the car. Lights are strung along the harbour, wires clanging in the wind. Johnnie helps her bundle him into the passenger seat and he immediately falls asleep. This is the other side of his fame. The recklessness, the assumption that someone will take care of him when he gets messed up like this. But why should it fall to Nell?

Back at Greenawn, she dumps him onto the bed, removing his shoes and belt. She places a small basin on the floor beside his bed, leaves him mumbling in his sleep. The halls are carpeted with a deep jade carpet that makes her want to take her boots off. A table in the hall is piled with boxes and packages, some stickered with recognisable brands. In the drawing room, the furniture is minimal but expensive, none of it comfortable. One corner has a customised unit with a turntable set up. There are shelves crammed with vinyl. Mainly jazz. Mingus, Davis, Coltrane (John but also – she's pleased to see – Alice). Music from the island. Hard to find stuff. The drinks trolley has an elaborate, international selection of bottles. She pours a dark peaty shot from a cut-glass decanter as exhaustion spreads through her. Tomorrow she'll message and ask what the hell he was going on about. Nell drains the glass and takes the fancy decanter as a souvenir. It rolls around the passenger seat on the drive home, glinting whenever the moon picks out its bevelled form.

57

Nell has spent the morning on the new Samhain request. Her fingers are crusted with glue and wayward threads. Sadhbh arrives with a note instructing Nell to go to Maman's office. After their last interaction, it feels like a ploy. It's meant to grate, she is certain. But Nell is ready and sprints up the back stairs.

The fire in the grate is lit, which is a surprise. The day is not especially cold and there has been so much talk of penury lately. Maman's desk is uncharacteristically messy. A handful of folders the same colour as the ones Nell has been given are tucked under a pile of papers.

– Good morning, Sister Nell.

A big smile and considerable breeziness. The opposite of the mood in the garden. It might be genuine, but Nell is not convinced.

– Hope you're keeping well this morning?

– You'll be happy to hear that I've nearly finished the piece.

– Oh I'm so glad!

She clasps her hands in joy.

– With no glitches, I should have it for you soon.

– What a relief! I was really starting to worry that you wouldn't have it done in time.

She laughs, an unconvincing chuckle. Nell presses her lips hard to her teeth.

– No need. Everything's on track.

– Can I see it then? I can't wait to get a look at what you've dreamed up.

The words rankle. Technically she could show Maman now. It's in decent shape. Possibly needs a little more detail. But no, let her wait.

– I'd hate you to see it before it's fully ready.

Maman offers a flatline smile.

– Well then, I'll wait. Patience is a virtue, as we all know.

– Is that why you wanted to see me?

– No. Actually, it's another matter altogether.

Maman tucks the smock neatly underneath her and leans back in the chair. This composure, deliberate or not, makes her appear regal.

– You know, it's hard to believe that the first people who approached me did so twenty years ago this very month. Just before Samhain. Isn't that a remarkable coincidence? I was younger and more pig-headed then of course …

Footsteps approach and there's a knock at the door. Maman motions for Nell to ignore it.

– Back then I was thoroughly adamant. I wouldn't allow it.

Nell doesn't yet follow but does not interrupt. The footsteps recede and Maman continues.

– I was too fixated on our privacy. And your book doesn't jeopardise that. But it's time to honour the Iníons' history in another way.

– You don't want the book?

– No, no, of course we do! I'm not talking about that; I meant the cameras … There was a time I would never have allowed them anywhere near Rathglas.

– Sorry – what cameras?

– The filming.

Maman drops the words in a low voice. Nell's confusion is evident, trying to put the words in order.

– Someone wanted to make a film about Rathglas once?

– Yes. You know how curious everyone seems to be about us. But, as you have learned since your time with us, Nell, we're not very mysterious at all.

– And you said no, naturally …

– In the past, yes, but times change, don't they? And it's such a generous offer. There's so much we could do with the money.

– What are you talking about?

– Your actor friend …

'Friend' was pronounced with specific emphasis. Derision was the word Nell thought of much later, when in that moment, sitting across from Maman, she couldn't think at all.

– Nick?

The mist cleared. Maman did not have to explain further, Nell already knew.

– Yes, he wrote to us. A very heartfelt letter, I might add. Saying how much he admired what we do. How communities like ours were a model for so many others, people that are trying to show there is another, more contemplative way to live. That he was your friend and that you had spoken so *warmly* of us to him. I was so touched to hear that, Nell.

– But I didn't tell him anything! Anytime he asked me about Rathglas, I told him nothing.

Maman picked at a thread on her robe, smiling.

– You meant well, and it's OK. You were trying to help.

– Now hang on. You asked me not to speak about what I was doing here. And I didn't. To anyone. And especially not to him.

That's why he thanked her in the pub. He'd used her name to get an in. How utterly sly. He'd made her look contemptible. Two-faced.

– So you've already agreed to this.

– I have.

– But what about the Iníons? Are they OK with it?

She ignored the question and pressed on.

– It's purely out of necessity, Nell. I explained the sanctity of Rathglas to him. That we have rules and regulations. That he cannot have the run of the place. He was very accepting of that. Respectful.

– You know better than I do that lots of the women are here precisely because they don't want to be in the world. Solitude is what they came for. And now this guy, this stranger, is going to be allowed in?

– Nell, I appreciate your concern, but please be assured that we're having a meeting tonight to discuss this.

– It sounds like it's already been decided.

– Discussed. Not decided.

The surge of anger passing across Maman's face is swiftly dismissed. She stands up, reaches for her shawl, turning off the lamp on the desk.

– Nick mentioned making a documentary, but I didn't take him seriously. Nor did I ever think you'd agree to it.

Maman steps out from behind the desk, tucking in the chair. Nell stands to face her. When they spoke about Muireann, she'd been shut down. But not now.

– Is this about money?

– Partly. And the outcome will depend on our meeting, of course. I will listen to everyone, I assure you. But you must understand that it's not just financial. I am focusing on our legacy. I don't think I need to tell you about the precarity of women's stories – the scores of women artists and makers and groundbreakers all blotted out of history. Our story can help people, Nell; what we have achieved here: self-sufficiency, harmony, peace. That should be known and that's what I'll be saying to my fellow Iníons. That our story, our contribution will be lost if we do not secure it now. Or someone else will find a way to exploit it. Surely you understand this?

– I thought the book you asked me to make was a legacy.

Her voice has risen in pitch. It is hard to keep the notes in check.

Maman gives her a pained look, as if she were stupid, or a child, or both.

– That project is for us, to be kept here. This is different.

– It doesn't feel different. An artistic, considered record for posterity versus a big glossy documentary that you're only agreeing to for the money? Jesus!

– Nell, I genuinely thank you for your forthright concern. You must know that I take it upon myself to be a buffer against the world for these women. To shield them and take care of them. Nothing matters more to me than the certainty that the Iníons and Rathglas endure. I will do everything in my power to ensure both survive.

She shifts in the chair defiantly. Resolute.

– I don't understand. And I definitely don't know if I believe you.

– This is not up to you, Nell. And in the end, frankly, it doesn't matter what you think.

They stare at each other. Nell feels a swirl in her gut.

It is clear Maman considers this the end of the matter. Nell gets up to leave but before she reaches the door, Maman is in front of her, the path blocked.

– Oh and Nell?

Nell waits, deflated. For now anyway.

– I won't mention your connection to Nick to the others, if that will make this easier for you?

She opens the door to show Nell out, a smile of pure victory on her face.

– *Suaimhneas*, Nell.

Nell stands in the studio for a long time, unable to move.
How stupid she's been, to be played like this. She must get
out of here before the meeting. The Iníons might blame her
for the actor weaselling his way in. They'll feel so let down,
and Nell can't bear to witness it. On the road home, she
floors the engine. Clips the mirror on a road sign. Pulls in
and tries Nick's phone, which goes to voicemail. For all its
high ideals, Rathglas – and Maman – was not incorruptible.
She thinks of all the time she has given to the group, the
admiration she had for their way of seclusion. And now
one person is dismantling it, and all of that trust, brick by
brick.

58

That night on the rig, the men play cards. When the dinner plates are cleared, a handful head to one of the bigger cabins. The man who ended up in the water remains in the sick bay. Cleary suggests they play cards to settle the nerves. He has a gift for poker. Cleaned up most nights. Money that means he could go home sooner. If he could make this a regular thing, he could keep the stints at sea shorter. The lads are good-humoured about it, and always pay up.

Afterwards, out on the platform, Cleary takes in the night. Only the perimeter lights are on, the ones blinking on the landing pad. Being outside highlights the distance. Smoking is banned but he huddles in to light the rollie, noise clanking from the vents. In the daytime, it's impossible to be out here without protective headphones. The wind whistles in the wires, a reminder of the singing bridge at home. That mad oul' wan who hangs around talking to it. Maybe the island isn't the worst place in the world. A deep drag, the bitter smoke circling his lungs.

She's there. And the lads from the boats. Jimmy. The hares and the cliffs. Banshla. But mostly Nell.

She's bound up in all that geography. He thinks of the sound; the way it filled up every patch of air. Like Nell. Distinct, intrusive. Hard to forget once encountered.

In her own detached way, Nell makes him feel safe. That unquenchable thing she has going on. Her own semi-permanent state of dissatisfaction. United by the island, the weather, the sound. Many things make them kindred.

The rollie goes out. A two-finger pinch to be sure it's spent. He takes out his phone.

Hey. Hope all's good. Work is grand. Long shifts, boring. Cleaning up at cards. Am sure you're busy but am back in two weeks. C.

He types two hearts. Backspaces. Inserts a heart. Deletes. Thinks again, imagining her, and dispenses with kisses and cardiac shapes. Instead, a solitary, definitive CLEARY.

59

The Iníons' meeting was held in the main dining room, all lit up with anger. Only a handful saw Maman's point of view. Arguing that a stranger among them compiling a book was already one kind of intrusion, but someone documenting their lives on camera was another. Sadhbh pointed out that there would be no control over their own narrative, and how Rathglas was represented. Aisling reminded them of the potential online noise, articles, hot takes. No chance of rebuttal. Judgement, humiliation. And then the pilgrims. Showing up for years to take photos or write on the walls. The money made some deeply uncomfortable. Others were driven by the ethical concerns about 'telling their story', given the years of isolation and adherence to privacy. It was showy and vain to want the world to know about this place. Bias was inevitable. The actor, and any producer or director involved, would all have their own agendas. This presented the very real possibility that they would be tempted – encouraged even, by the studio or backers – to portray the women as extremists. Sile was frank, outlining the mental health impact of such an intrusion.

Maman pulled out the ledger and pleaded with them about funds. Rathglas, she revealed, was not sustainable in the long-term without some infrastructural investment. Voices were raised. Things were said that could not be unsaid. No one could remember strife like this, clouding the air. When Maman left, whispered conversations continued. It would bring down on them the kind of attention they'd spent years trying to avoid. Some wondered whether this was about saving Rathglas, or something else entirely.

The women had ceded from society – from passports, jury duty, weekly supermarket shops, tax returns, pensions, from husbands and children – to make a life that pivoted around communion with each other. The world they had constructed worked because of its communal nature. They moved like swallows in a murmuration, united, unwavering.

Until now.

Maman's actions had changed that forever.

60

Muireann stops by the studio, having spent the morning in the cove. Nell moves a box of paints from a chair for her to sit and stacks the folders in the corner. Some pages are drying on a table and Muireann looks at them for a long time, not saying anything. It's barely afternoon but the late October gloom necessitates the lights being on. Muireann has brought Nell a fistful of Carrageenan moss and a small, scalloped shell. The lids of her eyes are pink, a spot is forming above her lip. The tallest of the Iníons, she looks smaller, as though her shoulders are being magnetically pulled to the floor.

– I still can't believe she's doing this.

Nell listens, sweeping up bits of fabric, confetti'd on the floor.

– Everyone seems so against it.

Muireann outlines a long list of objections and the collective unease at this encroachment. The bizarre idea that the actor is the right person to represent the ethos and history of their community. A man, and one who isn't from this island, or even this country. Nell herself cannot locate any overlap between the Iníons' way of life and his. Their reverence and abstinence, and his unfetteredness. How could he possibly understand these women; the significance of this female space; their rituals and motivations? When she started out as an artist, Nell directed a couple of short films, but even she wouldn't have believed she was equipped to undertake this.

– What I don't get is that we're not allowed phones or to watch TV. Any outside connection with the world is discouraged, yet this is OK?

Nell wishes she'd been upfront with Muireann earlier about her involvement with Nick. His questions about the Iníons. Admitting it now would make things worse.

– We've gone from you in the studio to a FUCKING DOCUMENTARY? How can that be?

– I never meant to cause any hassle by being here.

Muireann, exasperated, sighs deeply.

– No, sorry … you're fine. I mean, when we heard about you, we were anxious, but it's not the same. At least the book is *for us*. You GET us.

– Do you think it's more about money than legacy?

– I really don't know, but neither make sense to me. I mean, it's obvious we live on very little, but we get by … I'm trying to see her point of view. That there will be no legacy at all if Rathglas closes. But all I see is hubris and arrogance.

Nell is still furious at Nick. If he hadn't been able to use her name, he'd have given up. Or found another way. A ball of anger rolls in her gut.

– Maman had already decided. The meeting was a joke. No matter what any of us said, she had an answer to justify it. Her mind was made up.

– And there's no way to stop it?

– It's a done deal. He arrives tomorrow.

Nell is annoyed at her own foolishness. Nick had completely played her. Samhain is almost here. The end of this project, this commitment, all of these people – the actor, the women – that ultimately she owes nothing to. But she does care for Muireann and worries for some of the more vulnerable women. It's all the more painful to think she led him here. She may as well have thrown open the gates in the middle of the night and snuck him in.

61

The following morning, the dawn is raucous. Gales and five types of rain, which doesn't help with Nell's fitful sleep. Eventually she gives up, and leaves early for Rathglas, to get there before he arrives. It's less than two weeks to Samhain. In the studio she bends wire, dabs paint, trying to focus. To finish the book. And the final object: a crown. Often at the last stage of a work, she has to dig deep, try to locate the last well of energy. Her mother used to tell a story about the final week of her pregnancy with Nell, heavy and flushed. Labour started with cramps in her back and instead of resting, she spent hours rearranging the furniture while contractions danced up and down her spine. If only Nell could harness something of that now, a completist kind of frenzy. But today all there is, is the opposite; a sense of disconnection, worried that the Iníons will think she was involved with what's happened. She listens out for his car on the driveway gravel.

She takes in the studio that has been hers these past few weeks. It's a paltry space. The most unvisited room in a house. A large tapestry hangs on the studio wall, a communal piece added to by the Iníons over the years. It depicts a gathering, some sort of parade or party. Maman insisted it was hung in the studio as 'inspiration', as though another piece of art might expedite productivity. Nell hates it. The coarse fabric. The perfunctory workmanship in insipid colours. From the first day it has exuded something malignant, as though it had been stitched not in joy but under duress.

Even when her life is chaotic and asymmetric, order has always been a hallmark of Nell's practice. Each day, in the studio, she makes a point of giving the finger to the ugly tapestry. A reminder to do better. Nell lies on the floor, thinking of her own timelines, of life's small chronologies. Her birth, prolonged and painful after her mother's frantic nesting. Picking blackberries with other island kids, playing soldiers with ribwort, hiding in brambles, listening to ghost stories. Trying to train a rat to be her friend, her failed attempts to learn guitar. The first time her father let her down, made her feel small. The white heat of arguments in the house. Right about the time she is reliving her first period, pain undulating through her lower body and bleeding into all those towels, she hears it. The crunched arc of a car turning on the gravel.

Nell is up and makes her way to the corridor overlooking the driveway. He is alone, no film crew straggling after him. Dressed in a three-piece suit with a pocket watch, handkerchief and a pair of spats. A staggering ensemble she has never seen him in. Through the open window, the high tinkling note of Maman's laugh. Is that ... *flirting?* Peering out, the stance is at once recognisable as that of a confident, entitled man: wide-legged, arms crossed, nodding sagely while waiting for his own turn to speak.

The Iníons have lined up, at Maman's insistence, to welcome him. She takes up a spot at the head of the line, assertive and formidable, and – judging from the sparkle in her eyes – not immune to his handsomeness. Despite the armour of the suit, the actor is more reticent than usual, approaching the women with what looks like trepidation. Nell cannot tell if this is deference, fear, or an astutely choreographed performance. No doubt he has played such roles on screen before.

They move towards the vaulted lobby, walking in the direction of Maman's office. Nell waits until the noise and movement settles down before leaving. On the stairs, two novices giggle, starstruck.

He's likely getting the grand tour, and soon Maman will want to show off the cliff garden. Outside, the twine that holds up the hedges squeaks mournfully. The picnic table is neat, recently cleaned. The garden is deserted but they'll be here soon. Nell wanders to the furthest edge of the cliff. Not close enough to tip over, but the wind up here could lift someone of her weight easily. Deep breaths of the gusts rush into her lungs. Closing her eyes, a scene: herself fallen on the rocks below. Legs twisted in gymnastic angles, the pomegranate mess of her head, seawater turning maroon.

Not that such an end is an option. He might even admire the cinematic drama of it. How stupid she was to fall for it, ingratiating himself for an in to these women. Maman is the bigger let-down. She who had shunned the world and capitalism, who held disdain for transactional ways of living, now prepared to take film money and abdicate privacy. Nell has learned this lesson many times over. Never be surprised when people who claim to have principles end up reneging on them.

But she sees the fragility of it all now. How there are chinks. Everyone has something they're willing to trade. Disillusionment hangs, a rook on a wire.

PART FOUR

62

The actor is sequestered in the old chapel. Maman had the novices make up an old convent bed, trundling it across the garden. To appease the Iníons, strict rules have been established. He is not allowed to enter the main house unless invited. Nor is eating meals with the women permitted. For the first couple of days, he wanders the cliff garden, a small digital camera around his neck. No attempts at interviews or contact are made.

Nell heard he'd brought in hand cream, expensive tea leaves, chocolate, and had been passing them around. Trying to woo them with bergamot lotions, lemongrass tea and 95 per cent cacao.

Muireann and Maman are still not speaking. The Iníons are divided, those wanting to trust Maman, who has always guided them. Others who feel as Muireann does, trying to absorb the feeling. To bury it out of loyalty. Aisling claims she will never speak directly to Maman again. Rumours spread that others want to leave. The start of a schism. A fissure in the united front of Rathglas.

63

The chapel is freezing. On waking each day, Nick's bones constrict, curling in on themselves. In the tiny sacristy is an old kettle. The chrome is mottled. The lid doesn't quite fit. The sole plug is on a wall freckled with damp. Each day before plugging it in, there is a genuine moment of thinking it might be his last. While the water boils, the tiles of the portico are cold under his feet, but he stretches, does push-ups, feels his back muscles light up. Then, he retrieves the list of jobs for the day. Sadhbh never addresses him directly but leaves a list of chores under the door each morning. He's happy to help out. Especially if it means access to the Iníons for interviews.

He is allocated the worst jobs. Mucking out the pigs. Sorting compost and rubbish. Tending the waste bonfire, which he finds very satisfying. He holds off a couple of days before revealing his extremely green fingers. A gift gleaned from his mother, who could coax any vegetable from the stony plains where he grew up. He weeds and preps seed beds. Takes pleasure in making paper cones for bulbs that need to be put down and shows Muireann how to make green manure from other plants. For the briefest of moments, she looks impressed.

Nell passed him in the garden yesterday, throwing a look that clearly intimated he must never acknowledge their acquaintance. He doesn't want them to fall out, he likes her, is grateful to her for helping to make this happen. Maybe if he can get these women to trust him enough to talk to him, she might realise that the film is a good idea. In the meantime he'll focus on gathering some handheld shots and figure out the story later.

He's only been here a couple of weeks and is still trying to gain their trust. It's taken longer than expected. So far, only Sadhbh has agreed to talk to him on camera. What she had to say was rambling; a little scant on detail, not the meat he'd hoped for. During the day, he moves around, filming discreetly, scrolling back later to select scenes that might work as establishing shots. One particular Iníon shows up in much of the footage, in the background. Today she was hanging out washing but kept looking at the camera. Her face had a haunted, secretive look. As if there was something she wanted to say. In the dark of the chapel, he replays that look, over and over. The sheets billowing, white against her grey smock, a long pale curl, fallen lose from under a headscarf. It reminds him of something.

64

In the morning Maman is waiting in the studio. Her face set to mild irritation, as if trying to locate something she's misplaced. The early winter sun picks out dust in the air as she paces the floor.

– Good morning, Nell, I hope you're well?

– Fine, thanks … with three days to Samhain, I'm just trying to get everything wrapped up.

It's a polite way to indicate that this is an unwelcome interruption.

– Am I intruding?

Testy, rhetorical. Nell says nothing.

– I just want to run something by you.

Nell fidgets with materials, moving paint pots. Rinsing brushes that are already clean. Anything to indicate there's work to be done.

– I've been thinking about the documentary. It would be very useful for your actor friend to have some context. Some background on who we are.

– Can't he do his own research?

– Oh, of course he can, but to speed up the process, I thought you might like to show him your wonderful book.

– Surely you're not serious?

– But it would be so helpful for him to see what you've done.

– He can make his film, but I don't see why he, an outsider, needs to see the testimonies. They're so personal.

– They are, but then you've seen them.

She laughs, too quick.

Nell struggles to understand the loyalty to this man, and this new combativeness, after the weeks she's spent here.

– Tell me if I'm missing something, but didn't they tell you these things as a sort of unburdening when they first arrived at Rathglas?

– Yes. It wasn't mandatory … and I'll ask for their permission.

– Why *did* you ask for their stories, Maman?

– To help them, and to preserve the stories of all the people we've helped.

– Or so you'd have something on everyone?

– I really don't like what you're implying, Nell.

– Most of them probably would have said anything to get in the door.

– You really don't know what you're talking about.

– They told you these things so that you'd let them stay. So they could be safe. Not so that you'd expose them to the public. It's not right … you must know this? Do you think he'll be here doling out aftercare?

Maman jumps from her chair, furious, red-faced.

– I have never asked for a THING from those women. Not a thing. And what have I gotten in return? Very little. I don't want anything, but there's certainly no gratitude. Not a scrap. And lately, very little in the way of respect.

She sits back down, biting her lip.

– We turn no one away. We are home and hearth for so many.

Her voice cracks a little. Nell waits, wanting out of this conversation.

– I don't want to be involved, or for the Iníons to think I'm complicit. I just want to finish what you asked me to do and get back to my own work.

There's a pause, anger subsiding. Maman's redness fades. Nell takes a deep breath, willing the conflict to be over.

– Nell, it seems we both have our life's work, don't we? Art is yours. Rathglas is mine. We're more kindred than you realise, Iníon Nell.

The word hangs in the air, failing to dissipate. This is where it has been leading.

– I'm not an Iníon.

– No, and yet you are in so many ways. I've always seen it. From the first day you came here.

Her voice has softened. The words infused with a vaguely maternal note. Maybe she would still listen to Nell.

– These women rely on you, Maman. You need to talk to them. Ask what's best for them.

– They think of me now as some sort of scourge. I represent rules. You don't. You live another kind of life.

– You know that's not the same. Maybe the Samhain ceremony will help. A kind of healing for you all.

Maman faces Nell. For a moment it looks as though she's about to cry, or laugh, or perhaps answer some question still hovering on her lips. Instead, she pulls herself upright, flattening her mouth, seriousness returning.

– What we've built matters more to me than anything. But I'll think on your words.

Nell nods.

– *Suaimhneas*, Nell.

A final resolute nod and Maman is gone.

Nell, utterly drained, takes a break in the cliff garden. It's deserted under a shimmer of weak sun, the whole sky wide and grey. The table where she and Maman had tea weeks ago is strewn with fallen leaves. Chocolate shades, rust, congealing in the rainwater. A dead moth splayed out on the wood, and she picks absently at the wing.

The actor cannot be allowed that kind of access to the testimonies. It's not her battle, but there must be some way to resolve this. The horizon is a watercolour line. Out there on the ocean, ships are ploughing their paths. Containers packed with lush fruit, tankers of Gulf oil, cars from Japan stacked; seats shrink-wrapped in plastic. It is easy to forget there is a whole world away from this place. Places she has yet to see. Where she is not dragged into conflict not of her making. But it'll be done soon. She imagines herself far away. The sea growls, foam fizzing on the rocks. A lone dolphin surfaces in the bay below.

65

This new turmoil has cast a pall on the group. Tension fills the corridors. Two days to Samhain and Aisling busies everyone in the dining hall with tasks for the ceremony. An attempt to keep minds occupied and mouths shut. Garlands for the trees. Headdresses and sashes to wear over tunics. Nell has fixed the beat-up sewing machine in the studio and brought in bags of scrap material, leftovers from a textile project. Gold thread and bolts of green net. A roll of silk she'd paid too much for that didn't suit the piece in the end. Several spools of thread for the machine, in various blues and purple. She hauls the machine into the dining room. Nick appears behind the kitchen hatch. Chopping food and talking to someone behind him.

Well, that didn't take long.

Irked, the needle runs away from her, the fabric gathering in a mess of stitches. Nell yanks it out and makes for the door beside the hatch. The Iníons, gathered around the machine, watch as she goes in search of Sadhbh. All eyes follow her across the room.

– Hi Sadhbh.

She looks up, face smeared with displeasure. In all her

time here, she, and Rose, had remained consistently stand-offish. Before Nell goes on, Sadhbh turns to the actor.

– You – yes, you, I need you to go to the garden and pull veg for this evening.

– 'Pull veg'?

He repeats the phrase like a bad taste on the tongue.

– Carrots, parsnips. A few turnips. Oh forget it, take out the compost to the pigs. Go on now …

Nell often offered to help in the kitchen but was always turned down. That the actor is fully ensconced in the kitchen after less than a fortnight riles her. Not that she wants to peel spuds or stretch meagre amounts of butter across recipes. Nor does she want to become Sadhbh's confidante. The expedited trust is galling. That he has won factions of them over so quickly.

– Can I help you, Nell?

– Maybe. I have a question.

– I'm heading to the garden to get the veg that eejit didn't. Walk with me if you want.

It's difficult to tell how old she is. Skin ruddy but lined. Someone said she used to work in a café but had gotten ill. Nell can't figure out why she'd taken against her from the start. It's not just the outsider thing. Even those who keep to themselves nod politely when she passes them in the garden or corridors.

– Why is the actor in the kitchen – I didn't think he was allowed in the building?

A beat. Enough to indicate irritation.

– Do you know what it's like to make the same food, day in, day out? Stew. Soup. Spuds. It's tedious but I'm sure you know nothing about that.

Sadhbh hunkers down, pulling at the soil. Coagulated clumps of muck stain her hands.

– All I'm saying is—

– He knows how to cook. Says he's pretty handy at it. Seeing as I'm the one who's ended up running the kitchen, I'll take any help I can get.

– I'm sure it's a lot of work for you.

Sadhbh gathers up the carrots, tossing them in a basin. She struggles to get to her feet and ignores Nell's outstretched hand.

– Eleven years. That's how long I've been in charge of the kitchen. It's a bit 'loaves and fishes' at the best of times. Worse recently – which we won't get into now – but there's not much in the way of exciting ingredients. Quantity is what we have to worry about.

The wind is whipping up. Nell knows to be quiet, tucking her hair back into her hat.

– He seems to know what he's doing. So forgive me if I wanted a break. If I wanted someone else to have a go.

– I didn't realise how long you've been doing this. How hard it has been.

Sadhbh softens a little, even if this is calculated, aware of her own isolation and a need for allies.

– You know he's making dauphinoise later? To go with the fish Muireann caught. Dauphinoise! I ask you.

They laugh. It seems like such a ridiculous dish amid the very basicness of Rathglas's dining room.

– I wasn't in favour of it. Him coming here. But he helps carry stuff, chops wood. Knows how to handle a wheelbarrow. And that's without the dauphinoise. Maman says if he's here, we may as well make use of him. Anyway, I better get back to it. It never ends.

Sadhbh nods and moves back across the grass to the back door. Nell had never considered the miracles she performed with food. The difficulties of making it go far, of variety. Perhaps loyalty to Maman was about making sure she wouldn't have to fight for provisions.

Nell glances up and he's leaning against the back door, as if their conversation had summoned him out into the air. Smoking a rollie, he stares at her intently, before shifting his gaze away to the cliff edge. One more deep lungful. He flicks the crumpled butt onto the grass and goes back inside.

He might be ignoring her, or sticking to the cover story that they don't know each other. She doesn't want the drama either way. In an hour she'll be home. Samhain is almost here. The book is nearly done. Then it's over.

66

When she first arrived here, Muireann felt bloated with fear.
It filled up every cell. Lurked in her organs and bones. The
city had gotten too dark. The only people who stayed were
the ones who should have moved on long ago. Too old for
rollovers, for Friday to Sunday benders. Talking to
strangers at parties for hours about the Constitution, the
death of the planet, music that makes you cry. Rent on the
flat, small and cold as it was, kept climbing. On days when
it was colder in the building than outside, she would go to
the park up the road. In through its elegant gates and big
arch, to watch the ducks in the pond squabbling over bread
scraps. The benches were the old, original ones. Not the
ugly plastic ones you see everywhere. Sturdy oak and black
wrought iron, thick with gloss that glistened in summer.
Some days she spent hours there. The demographic of the
parkgoers shifting with the time. Mammies with elaborate
buggies, throwing back espressos from the hut near the
gate. The women in their fifties strutting past in pairs,
power-walking. Students on the grass passing joints and
bunking off early from classes in the college across the road.
When she had been coming here for a while, she noticed an

elderly woman, always in the same spot. Usually, meticulously made up, but there was always something not quite right about her. Once, she followed her and realised that the woman was homeless but went to great lengths to disguise this. Sometimes she still thought of her. The immaculate hair, the tailored jacket. Lip gloss in a peach shade. Where did she go every night?

Rathglas was home now. A place of contrasts. It made her want to live every minute while staying away from the rest of the world. Outside, she merely existed, moving through the days. Here, it was possible for her to thrive. It wasn't ever a utopia, but it had felt like all she'd ever wanted. Maman had changed all that.

67

For the last few days, there has been a rat in the cottage garden. Moving slowly among the plots, and out far too much in daylight. At first Nell thought it was a buck, but after it got near the back door, she noted the shape, the bulge of its gut, and realised it was a pregnant female. The creature moved in a dazed sort of way and didn't respond when she banged on the glass. By Thursday, a swarm of flies were following it. A large navy bluebottle sitting on its back, a grim harbinger.

The longer she worked at Rathglas, among the simmering tensions, the more her stomach contracted. The way it does when things start to pile up. Days when she feels like a blown candle. It happened a lot as winter approached. The change in season caused an unmooring. Instead of the sense of possibility in the first few months of the year, the end of autumn represented an impending, sustained dip in temperature. A winter that would stretch into six months. Months of the boats not running and deliveries not arriving from the mainland; of no tourists and the main street quiet. It used to be why Nell loved the place, but this year, after Rathglas, it felt like the tightening of a circle, as though she was being

262

stalked by the island itself. A desolate perimeter. For the next couple of weeks, she was tethered to things and people and commitment that she could not quietly exit from.

It was almost 1 November. Samhain, finally. The deadline would give some finality to the last few months. She was glad to be done with Nick. And sad, kind Cleary would be back soon, to routines and his uncle and rabbit corpses drip-draining in the bathroom. At times, she felt like Newton's cradle. A man at either end, and Nell as the metal orbs, hemmed in, struck, and struck again. An endless *clack, clack, clack*. One at each ear, talking in and out of her brain.

But she can't really blame them. If anything, it was the Iníons' book that made her realise the importance of her own work. She couldn't always understand their lives, but maybe they felt the same way about her? It certainly wasn't a life for everyone. Investing time in her art, living on next to nothing. The painstaking slog of it. But she liked the fact that the only person she answered to was herself. She desperately wanted that peace back now. The rhythm of working from dawn until nightfall when inspiration grabbed her by the throat. Meals skipped, not leaving the house. When she was at the last bend with the forest project, she began to notice a smell; garlicky, even though it was too early for the wild fronds. It worsened over a couple of days, until she realised the smell was her, unwashed, bedraggled.

All the projects she wants to make have piled up. Stacked like rocks around her. Anxiety snaking up her arms, across her chest.

So done with all this. DONE.

In the bath that night, a fourth gin warming her windpipe, she picks off the red varnish on her nails, watching the bloody fragments float on the surface. Cleary liked her nails painted, the actor didn't. The water has become cold and there are deep wrinkles on her feet, hands puckered. A message pings from the bedroom, she towels her hair and moves towards the phone. A shock.

Jimmy is seriously ill and has collapsed. Cleary will be coming home sooner than planned.

68

By the end of the week, there is no sign of the rat. Perhaps it crawled under the shed to expire. If Cleary was here, there'd be advice. How to put it out of its misery without taking a shovel to its tiny skull. She imagines him on the rig. Distracted. Worrying about Jimmy. She overheard the schoolteacher telling Cathal it was a stroke on top of the cancer. That things weren't looking good for him.

Inside Rathglas, the building has mice. Every evening, she carefully locks the archives back in their chest in the studio. As she does so, she sees yet another note from Maman, slipped under the door. A request to stop by the office. If this turns out to be about more work or again asking to allow the actor near the archive, she will leave for good.

Maman is bustling about. Face alert, slightly giddy.

– Come in, come in. Please sit.

This address always made her feel like a lap dog, but she complies.

– I know I mentioned it before, but have you had any more thoughts on staying with us the night before Samhain – with all of us? There's always a great buzz about the place. Things kick off the day before, once it gets dark.

The shift in mood. The warmth. It feels like an olive

branch. The thought of being here outside of work has never crossed Nell's mind. Every day, when she leaves, a tiny plume of relief leaks from her. Walking out through the gates, she's often felt superstitious about looking back. As if something awful might be waiting there for her.

– I appreciate the offer. Genuinely, but I have work of my own to get back to …

– I know it's all go with the Samhain celebrations, but it really feels special this year. Like we're marking a new era with our thirtieth anniversary. A rebirth. Goodness knows, we're in need of some recalibration.

Ryan's always throw a Halloween do. Tacky costumes, drunken apple-bobbing and a vaguely spooky playlist – 'Monster Mash', 'Thriller' – on the speakers. It's possible she'd missed Cleary there some years, in costume.

– OK, I'll let you know.

– This year feels different. And much-needed after all the, well, friction. I hope everyone likes the piece you've made. I can't wait to see it.

This is said with pride, but there's a small, elusive note of something less magnanimous.

– It would mean a lot to us for you to be here with us, Nell. Before we part ways.

The phrase is oddly adamant. Pleading almost. It's easy to imagine Maman as someone who is not used to being told 'no' in life. Perhaps this is unfair. Nell is curious about what the old convent looks like at night. How the sea sounds against the cliffs here. Out the window, over

Maman's shoulder, Nell can see the actor moving around the garden, bowl in arm, carrying whatever bounty Sadhbh has ordered him to retrieve from the earth. He stops talking to Aurora and, from his stance, it is clear that this is flirtation mode. That head tilt, the thing he does with his mouth. The young Iníon's face, glazed by the sun, says as much. When Aurora turns to go, Nell watches him watch her, wondering what he's thinking. If he feels victorious.

– That's settled then. I'll have the room in the attic made up. I'm sure you'd love a break from that draughty studio.

– The studio is fine, honestly. I've gotten so used to it.

– Wait 'til you see the view from up there. If the day is clear, the dawn is so magical. It makes me … well, sorry! I'm rambling on. We'd love to have you, if you'll humour us?

– Maybe. Let's play it by ear.

She runs through a packing list in her head, resolving to dig out the old hip flask and fill it. Burnished pewter, once the prized possession of her grandfather.

– Your labour – your work – means a great deal to us; I hope you know that, Nell.

It's good to hear her say this. Nell has put in a lot of hours, amid all the recent drama, it has felt as though Maman had lost sight of this. In some ways she envies these women. It would be so much easier to want the kind of life they lead. To want only that and for it to be enough. Her time at Rathglas has made her determined to seek out what she wants. More work. To stop resisting the long stark line of the horizon.

69

Cleary gets ready for shore leave, contemplating what life would be like if Jimmy was not in the world. Even though there is no mapped-out life waiting for him back on the island, he could build one. He has always liked feeling that particular kind of coldness in the bones. The damp squalor of the sea. *Salt in the blood, son, salt in the blood.*

Jimmy had promised him the house. No mortgage. He could fix it up. Proper insulation and triple-glazed windows. He'll look into a grant now that everyone cares about the environment all of a sudden. To keep out the rain and gales. Maybe even that sound. No one has found a fool-proof means of blocking it out.

Nell understands the island. The unspoken things everyone knows. When the basking sharks arrive, the best coves for night swims. The tides, the name of that pink hardy plant that anchors itself in the bad soil. Every sedimentary rock, the familiar arc of bad weather. The rare days of sun, white-hot rays bouncing off the lighthouse glass. Every moment lifted and sated, storing it up for the end-of-the-year greyness.

Cleary closes his eyes, figuring out how many hours he has left here. In the bunk above, his roommate snores, deep and guttural. The rig keeps doing its work. The machinery reminds him a little of the sound. The one he was so late to. Before Nell, all those years of being spared, for it to suddenly infiltrate, out of nowhere. It has to be connected, and yet he feels a deep shame for the way he shouted that night. Gunning the car, shirt flapping. The distance of the rig has helped. A realisation of stupid grievances. A hod of blame. He's tired of carrying it all. You can't outrun old hurts. It's time to slough it off. Choose something else.

70

The day before Samhain dawns grey and brisk. Nothing to indicate the celebration that lies ahead. Nell stops by Maman's office to hand over the crown for the ceremony, constructed from wire and fabric. Maman is adjusting some sort of headdress for tomorrow, mouthing handwritten words from a sheet of paper. Three candles flicker on the desk. The room smells of sage and burnt paper.

– Good morning, Nell. I really can't stop – there's so much to do. So it's finished?

Nell places the crown on the table. Makes a show of unveiling it.

Maman studies it, tilts it to the light. Nell is fully expecting a criticism, even a minor one but instead, she breaks into a huge smile.

– You've outdone yourself. I knew my instincts about you were right. Thank you, Nell. I'm so very grateful.

The metal was salvaged from an old performance piece. She wove old fabric scraps and flowers from the garden around it. In the centre sat the symbol Maman had drawn.

– Honestly, it's wonderful. A perfect way to celebrate our milestone anniversary. And the book – I trust it's nearly done?

– A few more tweaks. Just want to give it one final read-through.

– Thank you, Nell. For all your work. *Suaimhneas.*

Muireann shows Nell to the small attic space. Beside the single bed is a locker with a loose hinge, the door hanging at a slight angle. A tapestry, like the one in Maman's office, hangs on the wall. The scene – in dark shades, with hints of red – reminds her of Artemisia Gentileschi. A sword poised at a man's neck. A nightgown is laid out on the bed, fitted with a stiff sheet, and a single knitted blanket. The room is colder than the floors below, with a frugal air. The beams are exposed, blackened with age. On a small table sits a basin, a cloth and one of Sile's bars of soap. Pale mauve, scented with lavender from the garden.

– I'm afraid you'll have to head back down two flights if you want the loo during the night.

Nell accepts a small, scratchy towel, noticing a tic Muireann had recently developed. A sudden flicker of the eyelids that makes her appear vulnerable. It hangs there briefly and is gone.

A room alone here is a luxury. On the high ceiling, there is a spore of mould; inky, cellular. The peeling paintwork has a comforting kind of shabbiness. She thinks of all the Iníons who must have slept here. Before that, the convent patients. A collection of illnesses and fear. What moments had brought them to this room, that ceiling?

At the door, Muireann turns, hesitating. Too tall for the frame, she hunches over. It makes her look older. Nell beckons her to sit down on the bed.

– For what it's worth, I don't like these ceremonies. They seem so bombastic. Vulgar. For all the 'we're not like the outside world' talk, it seems weird to want such a big fuss. And no one really feels like celebrating after the recent hassle.

– Maybe a celebration will clear the air? Take the edge off.

– I think it'll take a lot more than a party to make everyone feel OK again.

Muireann has been the best part about coming to Rathglas. Nell will miss her. It feels like a long time since she's had someone to talk to. Someone who doesn't want anything from her in return.

– And what about you? Will you get back to your own work after this detour?

– Don't worry about me. I have a strong work ethic.

They laugh. Nell has a sudden urge to hear music. It feels like those long teenage hangouts in her bedroom.

– C'mere.

Nell puts her arms out and Muireann leans sideways, laying her head across Nell's lap.

– Will you go to the ceremony?

– I'm not sure attendance is optional.

Muireann sits back up and smiles.

– Here.

Nell hands her a small square, a cotton panel, embroidered with silk. Green and blue threads, in sea and sky shades.

– What's this?

– You always bring me gifts, so I figured I'd better balance the ratio a bit. Took me a while to figure out what to bring.

– It's beautiful. Did you make it?

– It was part of an old project. I had great plans to make this huge quilt. To be hung from Danu, as a sort of cloak. You remember the story of St Brigid's cloak? She once asked a king for some land to build a monastery and he said she could have as much land as her cloak covered. When she threw it down, it spread out and covered miles and he had to stick to his word. I always liked the story. Then life got in the way, so it never got finished.

Muireann turns the fabric over in her hands, pointing at the knots of thread.

– Is this a map of the island?

– Yes.

– Oh gosh! I miss so many parts of it. I loved swimming at Banshla strand when I first arrived. The place has such energy.

– I swim there all the time. You should come with me.

– You know I can't …

– Maybe you should just do it. March out through the gate, towel around your shoulders. I mean, who'd even stop you?

– Maybe I'll try it someday. You never know.

Nell tries to imagine staying here. Maybe there's comfort in order. Always knowing what's next. Muireann turns to leave, her mind somewhere else. Banshla strand maybe.

– I'll leave you to settle in – and thank you. For this.

She holds up the fabric, clutching it to her chest, and closes the door.

The last of the afternoon light begins to drain away. The pall between being too early for bed, but too late for much else. Maybe she should do one last check on the crown, but she cannot will her body down two flights of stairs. Tomorrow will be interesting if nothing else. Nell lies down on the Camberwick bedspread, a toothpaste-striped sheet underneath. Exhausted, under the black spore, she watches a spider on the ceiling. A fly in its web, wrapped tight, immobile. In the chapel outside, a bell begins to ring.

71

The old building seems quieter at night. Nell wakes, forgetting that this is Rathglas, convinced she is late for something. She swings her legs over the side of the bed, weary and disoriented. There is something wrong. Instead of floorboards, her knees are submerged in water.

It rises higher, climbing her thighs. Nell leaps off the bed, attempting to walk, dragging her legs through a wall of seawater. Steadily, it moves upwards, circling her waist. The room fills up more quickly now. Something snags her foot and then she is under the milky water. It is the same attic room, but the floor is further down, receding like an elevator. When she tries to surface, the ceiling rushes towards her. There is no way out.

Her chest begins to sting. The more she gasps, the more the flood fills her mouth with saline. Each attempt at expelling it is thwarted by too much water. A dam's worth. Lungs heavy as sacks, bursting under the weight of it.

Then she sees.

Hundreds of eyes in the water. All around her in the murk. Hands too, spindly, long-fingered. Attached to creatures that are foetal, unformed.

With each cough, panic swells. She tries to call out, but whose name can she say?

Little ones, little ones, what do you see?

Finally, stillness. Accepting that she has lost. Sinking onto shells and rocks. Down in the violet waves, the eyes stare.

Nell wakes confused, knotted in the sheets, salt on her lips. Opening the door of her room, she slips out, desperate for air. Down two rickety flights, she moves towards the fire escape exit and slips outside.

She has never been up here at night. This side of the island is rockier, more desolate, but the sound of the waves is comforting. The sea is black, the horizon a smudged line. The darkness is heavy, a kind of insulation. Far out at Cloughkeel Head the beacon twinkles, the sole illumination except for a handful of stars. A breeze cools her skin and carries a sound: singing. A series of rolling notes, words indistinct. Nell assumes they are readying themselves for the day ahead. The only certainty is the lateness of the hour.

She sits down on the iron step, thinking of the final adjustments to the book. The ceremony and what it might involve. Someone giggles in the dark below. A familiar sound she has made many times in the past: a flirtatious, *go-on-then* giggle. She already knows. A door closes quietly below, and she scans the grounds in all directions, waiting to see what it will give up. A minute passes, and there it is, an almost beautiful chiaroscuro: two figures hand in hand, standing close together. She waits and watches. The taller of the two figures bends in an almost balletic arc, leaning in for the kiss. The moon throws off a cloud and Aurora's face is suddenly illuminated against the actor; his back arched, mouth poised, vulpine. The pair move off towards the chapel, into the night. She can't blame Aurora, snatching such an opportunity, for closeness, for passion, for something long absent. All Nell can hope is that she knows what she's doing and keeps it from Maman. The metalwork pattern of the step is imprinted on her thighs, her arms are goose-pimpled, not just from the cold. A familiar tingle spreads over her skin.

72

The next morning, it happened, just as Nell knew it would. The feeling on the fire escape, now a flicker in the gut. A cellular alarm. Would it feel different here? Away from her own bed and the garden that would rest for winter. Those four familiar walls that she loves in spite of everything.

In an instant, she is up off the bed, clinging to the window. Watching. Listening. The Iníons never spoke to her of the sound, except for Maman. All these women from different places, it was inconceivable that no one among them could hear it. Of course she had always wanted to ask. Even Muireann. But it felt imprudent as an outsider, already trespassing on their privacy. She remembers the line of smocks hanging out the day after the mass bleeding. The echoes of hardier stains on the fabric, pale-pink smudges, heart-shaped.

Outside, Sadhbh is bent double in the vegetable patch. Novices are washing clothes in large tubs. Each immured in the rituals and routines of the place. Until the sound cuts through the air. The women halt what they are doing and, as if they were one. A trowel, a broom, discarded as they sweep towards one another, magnetic, in step. The circle expands so they stand side by side, arms linked in a ripple of bodies. Eyes closed, each expression intent and focused, they begin to sway.

Nell opens the window, expecting nothing but the familiar drone, but there is a low keening song on top of the sound. Nasal, plaintive. The women making their own chorus. The purpose is unclear: are they trying to commune with the sound or mimic it? Is it an attempt to replace the sound with a chord of their own? Two tracks looping in and around each other. She is filled with an urge to stand with them, sing alongside them. And cannot explain why. Maybe these women have impacted on her more than she knows. The sound seems to gravitate towards them, and they welcome it, commune with it. Nell cannot take her eyes from them.

Nell watches as the actor creeps slowly from the chapel, holding a small camera. He stays back, filming at a slight remove. This is exactly what he came for. The kind of footage that will secure backers, thousands in green-light funding. His face is full of wonder, almost childlike, gazing at the circle of ecstatic women, lost in something that does not include him. And that's when it hits her. For all his longing and curiosity, the certainty that he is in some way entitled to this place in all its profound mystery – it is clear that he can't hear the sound at all.

73

The day of the ceremony dawns purple. A rash of scarlet over the bay beyond Rathglas. During the night, there'd been movement and hurried footsteps. Occasional bursts of singing. Nell hadn't slept well, waking repeatedly. She tried thinking of an old project, as she often does when sleep will not come. The ghosts of old work come back to haunt her. It was a troublesome project from the start, but she still hopes it will happen one day. A series of underwater statues of gods of the sea, Norse, Roman, Celtic.

Too ambitious. Sourcing the right material would be difficult. Marble, ideally, but such an expense. It would only happen with backing. And the small matter of researching the safest way to secure them to the sea floor suggested costs might be considerable. Maybe Billy would help with a trip out to Dodder Bay to check the depth.

It is the custom every Samhain for the Iníons to fast, so the kitchen is silent. No heady porridge smells, or stewed tea humming in the tin boiler. A fresh Iníon's smock has been left folded on the chair by Nell's bed. The gesture is surely one of kindness and inclusion, but could be construed as an act of complicity. Of making sure she does not stand out from the rest of them on this sacred day. Pulling it on, she notices how thin her arms are. When this is all finished, she'll have to take better care of herself.

Nell picks up the book, scraping a speck of dried glue off the spine. It's hard to believe that it's finally done. All that awaits now are her own notebooks. Maybe she'll finish the cloak for Danu. The one she told Muireann about. She will miss her thoughtfulness, their talks. Waiting to see what gifts she's brought from the sea. Nell is happy with what she has created here but knows she won't miss the place. Or the menopausal boiler, the smell of damp and dust. It won't be so easy to give up the view, however, the endless sweep of blue.

Nell carefully wraps the book and makes her way to the stairs.

At noon, the chapel bell tolls, announcing the start of Samhain. The first day of winter, a festival of the dead. Nell thinks of her mother and grandmother. The ghosts of all the women who passed through this old convent. The lost souls who came to Rathglas in search of something.

The main ceremony will begin later when darkness falls. Until then, there is group prayer and reflection. Aisling and Aurora are singing harmonies. The bonfire near the chapel will be lit at dusk. The bell tolls a deep sonorous song. Nell adjusts the smock, fastening the high, tight button at the neck. She closes the door, taking the fire escape to the cliff garden. More Iníons emerge from the building below, moving among the cabbages and the neat rows of potted herbs, past the compost heap and beehives. In rows of two, a sea of smocks, in grey and slate, move towards the chapel.

A gull circles above, its call singing against the chime.

Nell ducks into the weed shed, hoping to find Muireann, but she is nowhere to be seen. Retracing her steps, she falls in behind the women, focusing on the horizon, struggling to make itself seen through cloud. Artists are meant to eschew hierarchies, but if she was forced to choose only a handful of colours to use forever, she would choose the island's spectrum of blue and green. Up here, purple dominates. But after today, there'll be no more of this. The thought of going back to her own life lifts the corners of her mouth. After the ceremony, she'll ask Muireann to climb down to the lobster pots one last time. To scavenge something together as a souvenir.

Outside the chapel, the Iníons look docile. Muireann raises a hand and beckons them. No one speaks as the wind spreads itself over the sound of the bell. The Iníons line up in circular rows, wreaths of greenery and ribbon on their heads. The noonday sun gives the sea a slick sheen. The air is cool, some of the women shudder in their paltry smocks. Candles in glass jars fill each corner of the garden, some hung with rope. Once more, the women begin to sing. The same song that echoed down the corridors last night. A tune practised for weeks.

Their voices get louder, bodies bending in time to the rhythm. Up close it feels more sinister somehow. Each throat united and filled with the same strange tune. Words in the old language, the consonants harsh. At first, Nell thinks it's a hymn, or some sort of anthem, borne of their community, but soon she recognises it as one of the island's ancient folk songs. Muireann doesn't sing but listens with eyes shut.

The effect is one of disorientation. Like the woozy feeling before fainting. The ground seems to rise and swell with the notes. Each tone hanging heavy in the enveloping air. The wall of Iníons parts and Maman emerges, wearing a gilt headdress of violet stones. Her smock is violet, a deep shade. At the chapel door, she turns to face the crowd, gesturing for the singing to quieten.

– My fellow Iníons. Welcome to this glorious Samhain day! A day like no other! To offer gratitude for all we have; for the bounty of our animals and crops; for our shelter from the elements despite our isolated spot.

Her words are greeted with clapping and enthusiastic shouts.

– Today is a day for celebration, for sustenance that will carry us through winter.

– We all know, sisters, that there are people outside this gate who do not understand us.

The women respond with jeers. Maman is buoyed up, revelling in the performance, in the captive enchantment of the novices.

– They think we're unhinged. That we are delusional!

The Iníons laugh with her, clucking, mimicking her ridicule.

Nell, uneasy, tries to catch the gaze of Muireann, who is in the front row, less ebullient.

– They condemn us. Discriminate and mock. It is they who are out of touch. Too far removed from the land and the seasons.

Muireann's mouth seals itself in a straight line. The other Iníons, in contrast, are swept up by Maman's energy, hooked on every word.

Nell has never seen Maman so impassioned. Cheeks flushed; head held high. There is something almost militaristic about her stance. A victorious general commanding the troops. Emboldened. It's as though the last few weeks had not happened. She is the leader she used to be and the Iníons are behind her again. Watching the scene, Nell feels they will do anything she asks.

– The sound has called us here to live alongside Danu. To live in harmony and oneness. In turn, she waits for us, for all time.

The pulse of the bell in the tower quietens A stilled metal heart.

– She is the earth and the water. She is life. We need no other for we have been summoned.

Maman raises her hand, and the crowd grows silent. There is no sound except for the sea wind.

We need no other! We need no other!

– Under her cloak, all is love and protection.

Nell is startled at the mention of the cloak. The Danu/Brigid project that never was.

– She keeps watch over the land and the water that surround us. That give us nourishment and protection. In all of this, she asks so little of us.

Livestock in the nearby pens shuffle. A large sow totters up to the gate to take a look.

– I ask you all today – what can we do for her …

A single drum starts to beat at the end of the garden. The Iníons join hands and begin to sway. Maman sounds a long low note, like a tuning fork, and the women pick it up. The note rolls on and Maman returns to the speech. Nell looks around to the other Iníons. Each head is bowed, eyes closed, the single note drones on.

– … and all the goddesses of *El Mar, Oké Osimiri … The Sea, An Fharraige*.

Behind Maman the chapel door swings open, six novices walk out, carrying candles in a tight formation. The Iníons change key, the note rising up, voices louder. A figure in their centre rises above all the others. The actor walks between them, on his head is a crown. The one Maman asked Nell to make.

The Iníons gasp. A whirl of chatter goes up. Nell looks at Muireann, who looks alarmed.

– Listen, sisters! We offer Danu our total commitment … let us sing.

Maman gestures to the Iníons, urging them to recommence their song. Some stay silent.

Rose and Aisling have stopped singing but are still holding the hands of those either side of them. Sile has a wild look in her eyes. Sadhbh, chanting the note over and over, beams up at Maman. Nell looks back to the actor, trying to figure out the incomprehensible nature of the scene. His head tilts upwards, a smile splayed on his features.

He's enjoying this. She spots the small camera in the centre of the crown, with another on a string around his neck.

– We offer Danu our undying worship … we must prove our devotion! Have we not toiled, my fellow Iníons? Have we not suffered? Yet, there is nothing we would not do for Danu. To her we offer all we have … and ask for absolution.

The actor flexes, at home in the part. As if this act of adoration is for him.

– Danu resides alongside the Nereids, deep down in the holiest of places … the place of rebirth. Only water will wash away all our sins and show her that we are committed to her, and the sound that is her voice, forever. Come, my daughters! *Teacht liom, mo Iníonacha!*

The novices nudge the actor and the group begins a slow procession towards the cliff ladder.

– We dedicate our prayers to her … *sios go dtí an fharraige*. Down to the sea, sisters, down we must go!

Maman is in full swing, arms windmilling, pupils dark. The women keep singing. Rhythmic, high-pitched, following the six novices towards the top of the cliff.

Each Iníon waits their turn to descend the ladder, hair billowing. The singing reaches a frantic level of fervour.

Behold, behold your blushing bride
The spitting, seething, foaming tide
The embrace of the deep, black sea
Together for eternity

The tone shifts, inching towards the macabre. Three novices descend, then the actor, followed by Sadhbh and Aurora, Sile and Aisling, and Rose and Ebele. Each moves backwards down the steps, like divers jumping into the blue. Nell searches for Muireann, whose alarm has turned to anger. The wind is merciless. It whips the smocks, an inappropriate choice for tackling a ladder in strong gusts. But Nell can see that there is no opting out now. Below them, the tide rolls closer in queasy increments, teasing the shore. Maman continues, fully warming to her subject.

– In water, we are reborn! In water, we pledge our loyalty forever!

– *At death of sun, and dark of year*

– *Our harvest hymn we pray you hear*

Because she is not an Iníon, Nell will be last to descend. A girl ahead of her misses a step and shrieks. Nell steps down next. The paint on the ladder feels more cracked and brittle today, scratching her hands. They keep going, a plumb line of bodies. On reaching the shingle, the cove offers little shelter. Lobster flags and buoys bob in the bay. Two Iníons help Maman onto a large rock, better positioned to project her sermon.

– Danu, goddess of the seas around our island! We come as supplicants and ask you to give us new life.

She gestures for the singing to recommence, conducting with one hand, the other outstretched towards the horizon.

– *May health and bounty be our share*
– *This gift we send to you with care*

The notes climb. The Iníons move towards the shore, barefoot on the shingle.

– We will be reborn in the waves – Chalchiuhtlicue! Sedna! Nāmaka! Hear our golden song, our silver notes!

Sile and Ebele join the novices and lead the actor away from where Maman stands. Towards the stake.

– Beloved daughters, we will prevail!
– *Danu, Danu hallowed mother*
– *Take the hand of our dear brother*

The Iníons negotiate about what to do next. Cowed a little by fame, but also fearful. There are whispered discussions. Muireann tries to approach but cannot get through the gathering Iníons. Two of them push her back. Sadhbh grabs her wrist as the novices position the actor against the stake. They bind his hands behind his back, spine pressed to the stone, waves already moving upwards. More Iníons move into the water, waves swilling around them.

– SING, my sisters! Louder! Danu can hear you!
– *Fruit of earth, seed of clay*
– *Libations on this sacred day*

Groups of women huddle in the cove, some on the shore, others in water, smocks spread on the surface of the waves.

Nell notices faces she has never seen before. The noise brings curious gulls, their squealing above mingling with the singing below, bouncing around the cove, a sinister oscillation. Nell waits for the frenzy to calm down, for Maman to stop, for someone – anyone – to say 'Enough!'

– We show you the depth of our love with this offering.

– *Libations on our sacred day*

The waves move fast, slamming on the angular rocks, onto helpless bodies. The furthest Iníons wade into the slanting waves, still pushing out the notes of the frantic song. The younger novices look frightened. A handful of women have stopped at the shore, others continue to step off into the waves. At the stake, the actor is already waist-deep. The waves keep coming.

– *Together for eternity!*

– Maman! What the hell is going on? Can't you see how dangerous this is? Someone's going to get hurt.

Muireann looks from the women in the water back to the woman on the rock, unable to move.

– *Together for eternity!*

Maman ignores the entreaty, addressing the Iníons again.

– We thank the earth for all that we have and all that we are!

The women break off singing to chant:

All that we are, all that we have!
All that we are, all that we have!

The waves move over the higher rock in the cove and rise up the stake.

The actor's face betrays the first hint of alarm. He swallows, trying to gauge the potential height of the incoming tide, now dancing just beneath his ribcage.

– OK, OK, I've gotten some footage, we're good. Can someone untie me?

– Let him go, Maman!

Muireann moves towards the rock, shouting.

– *Behold, behold your blushing bride*

– *The spitting, seething, foaming tide*

Maman picks up the refrain of the song sung by the Iníons, who are now nearly chest-deep in the waves.

– Stop this! For Christ's sake.

– With this offering, we beseech you to be kind to us, with the weather and harvest. Steer storms and gales away from our haven. Ensure our longevity!

– *The embrace of the deep black sea*

– *Together for eternity!*

– Make them stop, Maman! Come back in here – Sadhbh! Aurora – Please, get out of there.

The novices are crying. One faints, falling to the stones on the shore before she can join the other Iníons. Shouting, Nell grabs Síle's wrist and draws her back, looking helplessly at the women wading further out. The tide rushes in, white breakers around waists and hips. Maman, distracted by Nell's efforts to call the Iníons back, does not see Muireann rush towards her. A hard shove to the waist and Maman is falling. On the shoreline rocks, she sits up dazed. On her forehead is a large gash. She is silent for the first time since they left the clifftop. Red fury on her cheeks. The Iníons in the sea gather their smocks and Muireann calls out over and over, fighting to be heard above the wind, her throat hoarse.

The tide comes faster now and the actor calls to Nell, water swilling around his shoulders. Helplessly she watches Sadhbh and Rose ready themselves, waiting to give themselves to the water. One big swell covers Nick before subsiding, but it won't be for long, she knows this. Muireann is shouting to the Iníons, who are being swept back in by the incoming tide. The novices are wailing.

A decision. Nell kicks off her boots, dives in fully clothed and thrashes against the waves towards the Levinson Stake. Water fills her ears and the singing sounds more distorted, like a wail under water. The cold is unbearable, numbing her limbs, but she pushes on, swims for her life, for his. Some of the Iníons turn back at Muireann's urging. The realisation of what's happening settles on the actor's face as she works at the knots, trying to gulp air. The freezing water slows her hands and gulls swoop just above her. A huge surge lifts her off her feet and washes over his head, longer this time. One more knot, *come on!* Suddenly the rope gives, and the actor kicks free. They are thrown back towards the shore by the tide.

In the midst of bodies climbing up the shore, Maman is upright now, a rock in hand. In one swift gesture, she brings it down on Muireann. The Iníons gasp, horror-struck. The singing stops. Finally, for the first time since the procession began, there is only the sound of waves, wind and the birds. Rose and Ebele rush to Muireann, sitting shocked and bleeding. Aurora pulls off her damp headscarf and covers the wound. More Iníons return to the shingle, collapsing in exhaustion. Nell wades in to help the last few stragglers. Nick lies on his back, spent, coughing. All that can be heard is the furious waves and snuffled, quiet sobs.

– Are you OK? Is anyone hurt?

Nell moves around checking. Aisling and Sile hold on to each other, shivering together on the stones.

The women tend to Muireann, who is silent, a streak of blood moving down one cheek, her temple pulsing with the promise of a bruise, or worse. They sit for what feels like a long time, not speaking. Rose and Ebele move up and down the beach searching, looking back to each other, and Nell realises they're looking for Maman, who is nowhere to be seen.

– You OK?

Nell places a hand on Muireann's arm.

– I feel stupid. This got way out of hand. I should have said something earlier.

Out of the corner of her eye, Nell sees Aurora move towards Nick and wrap her arms around him.

Muireann stands up, leaning on Nell, dazed.

– Jesus. What is she doing up there?

Aisling points upwards. Quickly, determined, Maman has started up the ladder, ignoring the calls of the women below.

The Iníons, Nell and Nick follow her bewildered gaze.

– Someone go after her, quick! Maman! Come back!

They watch as she moves upwards, finally disappearing over the top.

– Where is she going? Rose, we have to get back up to the cliff.

Heavy rain clouds are starting to gather, the day immediately altered. They must get out of the cove. Aisling and Rose climb the rungs, more Iníons behind them, others struggling to find the strength after what's happened.

The wind grows stronger. Nell looks at the cliff and Maman is holding something in her hand, singing or speaking, the words lost to the gusting breeze. The Iníons pull one another up, scrabbling to gather themselves.

Nell is startled that Maman is nowhere to be seen and grabs Muireann's arm.

– Where is she?

– We have to hurry … C'mon, everyone! Let's go!

More Iníons make for the ladder. But all too quickly, up on the cliff, they see smoke. Maman has lit the Samhain bonfire.

Muireann urges the women up the ladder and will not leave until everyone is off the beach.

Nell helps the actor towards the ladder, feet struggling on the jagged stones.

The chapel bell begins to ring, slow and ominous.

– Look! Oh god!

Sile cries out, frantically gesturing to the clifftop. Sadhbh falls to her knees.

Against the slick, grey sky, Rathglas is burning.

74

Rathglas burned until dawn and smoke could be seen all over the island. Wooden beams crackled until the fire loosened them from the joists. The wind made it worse, flames dancing in sickening orange streaks. The kitchen wing went up first. The grand front door and the parquet tiles Nell crossed on that first day were lost. Every so often a creaking groan would indicate another collapse somewhere in the building. Cinders floated on the breeze. The smell carried across the land.

The Iníons worked all night. Dragging beds and clothing outside from the lower dorms, rescuing perishables from the stores. Someone even managed to grab the tapestry off the wall of Maman's office, but the rest were lost. Half the building remained standing. The outhouses and chapel survived. The frightened animals lowed and kicked up a fuss. If not for the fact that the breeze was blowing in the other direction, the garden and all the crops would have been torched. Within the hour, islanders arrived on tractors, in vans. Billy Butler took the gate off its hinges. All through the next morning, they worked. Heaping buckets of water onto the flames. Hooking up garden hoses. Doing all they could to bring the blaze under control. When it was finally out, the stench caught in the throat. The smell of centuries-old timber. Black, sodden, with odd wisp of smoke. Ash falling in grey fragments.

The islanders and Iníons stood side by side, exhausted. Local women brought tea and sandwiches. Cathal from the mini-mart handed out drinks and chocolate bars.

When the day finally broke in varicose shades, there was numbness and anger. Some novices knelt on the grass, praying. On an upturned wheelbarrow, Nick smoked a rollie, a blanket around his shoulders. A local woman offered him a bottle of water, which he slugged down.

Nell sat next to him, and he offered a weak smile.

– Some night, huh?

The famous eyes still pinched with fear. The sodden crown lay on the ground nearby.

– How are you doing?

– Shockingly, I've been better. What the hell was all that about?

– Did you know in advance? What did Maman say to you?

– She explained Samhain. Told me the ceremony is also a bit of a spectacle. A night off for them all. Because of the anniversary, she wanted to ramp it up a bit and I could join in. I just played along with the crown stuff.

– 'Ramping it up' is one way of putting it. One for the memoir, maybe …

He sucked down on the smoke. For the first time, Nell noticed the deep lines on his jaw. Age encroaching on his face.

– I'll say. What is that pillar thing anyway?

– The Levinson Stake. They used to tie heathens to it.

– Good to know …

He smiled grimly, gesturing to the crown on the ground, and then raised the small camera around his neck.

– At least I've got a record of it.

– That thing waterproof?

– I figured the damp gets into everything around here, so I came prepared.

– The police are on their way over from the mainland. They might want to see that.

The sun was higher now, a honey shade above the sea. Terns swept overhead making a racket, irritated at sharing the dawn.

They sat in silence, watching a man rake up ashes.

– What will you do now?

– My agent wants me out of here. She's already organised a flight. That mini-mart guy is giving me a lift to the ferry.

– And that's it. That's you gone.

– That's me gone.

Muireann calls from across the garden, where she is folding blankets and clothes, assessing what to keep. Nick takes her hand and she squeezes it back.

– So long, Nell.

75

After Nick departed and Maman was transported to the mainland came the worst storm in island history. Ferry sailings were cancelled for two days. Ryan's closed its doors for the first time in its history. No fisherman ventured out. Cows were herded into barns. In each house, every lamp burned all through the night.

The lighthouse beam swept on, a spectre of light out on the waves.

When it eventually stopped, all that was left was the same song of wind and sea. Back at the cottage, Nell gathered food from the garden, pulling up all the root vegetables, bunches of green scallions. She tipped green beans into old punnets, the wood mottled slightly with mould. Courgettes, fat turnips, beetroot, squash. The greenhouse emptied. She carried planters of herbs, a small bay tree, a bin-liner of wild garlic. Inside, she emptied the laundry press, shoving towels and sheets into pillowcases. All her bowls and cutlery. It took several trips to fill the car.

The road out to Rathglas was plagued with potholes and the plates on the back seat rattled furiously. The big gate was leaning against the wall, thanks to Billy's handiwork, and the air was still filled with the bitter scent of singed wood. A couple of news reporters stood at the gate, negotiating with locals who had put up a makeshift barrier. A helicopter from one of the mainland stations swooped around, with a cameraman hanging out of it. There were drones everywhere, collecting news footage.

Half the building was a blackened shell. Some of the dormitories were damaged. Most of the east wing survived, ironically the dampest part of the building.

Despite the damage to the kitchen, the large range is still working. Muireann greets her warmly, wearing a pair of trousers and a man's shirt. Some Iníons are without smocks, dressed in an array of donated clothes.

– Wasn't sure we'd see you again …

– Just wanted to make sure you're all OK. And to check on the studio …

Still standing, barely. Sadhbh appears and offers tea and a slice of shop-bought cake.

– So what now?

– I don't know. We'll try to rebuild, of course, but that will take time. And money.

– I'm so sorry.

– The islanders have offered us timber and there's a couple of lads who say they'll rewire the place for free. Do a bit of plastering. That kind of thing. I don't know where the deeds are, or if there's any insurance, but unlikely, I'd say.

Nell's phone buzzes in her pocket. Muireann hands her a bucket of peelings and they move towards the animals, ducking under clothes on the washing line, sleeves stained with residual soot.

– I can't leave, you know. Not after everything. There'll always be women who need this place the way I needed it.

Nell wouldn't have expected any other response. If she's learned anything about the Iníons in her time spent with them, it is their remarkable perseverance and ability to survive on very little. The sheer indefatigability of the life they've chosen. It makes sense to rebuild. The walls are charred, but the principles live on.

– Will you take over?

– Take over?

– You know … steer things along. Steady hand on the tiller and all that.

– In case you've forgotten, someone being in charge is what caused all this.

They feed the pigs in silence. Muireann fills the water trough.

– How is everyone doing?

– Rose and some of the others have left. Can't blame them.

– Why d'you think she did it?

– I've been here a long time and all I can say is that it gets lonely but you can't blame geography or isolation … Do I think she lost her mind? No. She knew what she was doing. In the same way she said yes to the film for the money.

Rathglas was definitely some kind of obsession. Maybe she felt she was losing the run of the place and had some warped desire to hold on to it, at any cost. Even if it meant this …

She gestures towards Rathglas. Nell contemplates the suddenness of it all. The implications of Maman's actions.

Near the benches where they used to gather, Aurora and Ebele are trying to erect another washing line, doing laundry in cycles to wash out the burnt smell.

– What about you – what will you do now she's gone?

– I've a car outside, full of stuff you can have.

– You're leaving the island?

– Not sure yet. I think so. Nothing to do with any of this … I've just been here too long. It'll do me good to get away. For my work, my head …

– For what it's worth, it's been great to get to know you. I hate that it all went like this … but I hope you won't forget us.

– How could I? And I haven't gone yet. Come on and give us a hand. That sack of wild garlic won't carry itself.

– How about a joint for the road?

– Deal.

76

Nell drives out through the gates just as the clouds open. Potholes fill up, a donnish shade. It is typical November weather, cold sheets of water filtering the light. The joint helped settle her head. She floors the clutch over bumps, urgent, restless. Longing to be away. To pack the last few boxes. On the seat, her phone pings: A missed call from Cleary.

She listens to his message while turning the key in the door, greeted by the fetid tang of the bin. On the mat is an art magazine she meant to cancel and the *Island Gazette*. She flicks to the death notices and obituaries, which her mother used to read, a habit she has inherited. Scanning the list, she spots the listing for James 'Jimmy' Cleary, repeating the arrangements Cleary just outlined in his message.

Later, she would learn he left Cleary his house. And all his money. Wads of cash double-bagged in plastic bags in the coal shed so his creditors wouldn't find it.

I'll be back this weekend for the funeral.

So much has happened between them.

Would it be OK to call over at some point?

The island is forever changed. The year irrevocably churning into the past.

77

On her last night, Nell stays up late to pack. In one room are all the things she wants to keep and will send for. She's told Billy he can redistribute the furniture if anyone wants it, or burn it as firewood. The cottage looks different now, a life emptied out. How quickly a house reverts to anonymity once personal effects are removed. Her mother's rosary beads hanging on the mirror. An expensive candle she has never lit. Books piled floor to ceiling.

It's cowardly to avoid Cleary. Tomorrow, Jimmy's coffin will be carried into the small church, watched by his nephew in a black suit, two different shades. A thin pencil tie. By the time he steps forward to cast a fistful of soil into the grave, Nell will be gone. She imagines him in the pub afterwards, muttering, *thank you*, over and over, after each *sorry for your loss*. Watching the door, searching Ryan's for her face.

He will be OK. She knows Muireann and the Iníons will be too. It will take the rest of the winter to let the last few months settle; to see what can be taken from it. If she has changed in any way.

And then, what often happens at the most inopportune time, an idea shows up.

The next piece of work.

A triptych of three figures. Each representing a woman who wants to live her life as:

pure fire

an artist

a rolling wave

Unbound by the contours of an island.

She will place these versions of herself in boxes. Post them overseas. Far from the pick-and-mix stones of familiar beaches. To new places.

The labels will read:

Every city in the world but here.

Three Nells.

An Triúr.

In the name of the Mother,

the Daughter,

the Holy Danu.

78

The morning breaks orange and blue. Nell heads for the highest hill on the island one last time. Only fishermen or new mothers are awake as she moves upwards. Longing for a certain kind of elevation. To absorb every rock and blade of grass. The hemispheric sweep of Dodder Bay, Cloughkeel Head beyond it, Greenawn and Banshla, the sea rushing to meet them all, dappled with glitter. From here, Cleary's cottage resembles a milk carton. It's too far to see the windows where she hovered with longing, watching him slump into his loneliness. The meagre hedges that shelter it. The breeze blocks he tried to make a barbecue on. The trees beyond, engaged in crown shyness. The diplomacy of the forest. Maman once said that women are the dendrochronologists of the world. Nell wasn't sure what she meant, but assumed it was about time, or that women were the guardians of history. Maybe it was about the repetition of life, the concentric nature of living in a place that is small, and so distant from everywhere else.

Cleary will likely move into Jimmy's house. He'll find comfort in its 360-degree views, a carousel of the sea. Ghosts in every room. The view of Rathglas, only visible if the rain holds off and the clouds aren't low. On clear days, it's possible to make out the high spire of the chapel, which survived the fire. The ladder down to the cove is still there. She thinks of Muireann hauling in buoys, the little lanes of coloured flags. The possibility of blue lobsters lurking in the pots, the clacking of crabs in a bucket. Scouring the shore for glass or pottery smoothed by the waves. Nell might write her a note to find. Ask one of the fishermen to throw the bottle into the sea when the current is right.

The winter sun washes across the grass tufts, pouring rays into her mouth. Each time she tilts her head up, heat spreads over her face. Liquid gold seeping out of pores.

From up here, she can see the road to her cottage. The sharp bend, not the house itself. In a way, she is glad. It would be painful to take one final look at the garden that took years to build. One day she will replicate all that green in another corner of the world; in a place whose palette is more than cobalt, moss and coal. On a balcony, maybe. But she cannot live far from the ocean. Seawater runs through her. Brine in each follicle.

Above her, a mass of meringued clouds, ready to burst. The purity of it. It would be impossible to comprehend a life that does not include this view. One which she has taken for granted, and occasionally cursed. What could the future be, without all this saturated liquid air, the comfort of drizzle, the songs to be heard in the wind.

I'm going.

That's what Nell told herself for years. Away from this

metronome place. Always on Sunday nights, when the dark closed in and another week loomed with no newness to it. A calendar of old-time lives inside her.

She craves heat and light. Only the diurnal. Birdsong. Flowers that don't close their petals.

To rely only on herself.

No ties, no restless seas, no damp, heavy particles in every inch of this place, no wind galloping through the forest, its own woodwind section. No hierarchies high on a clifftop, no distractions from making the work.

And the sound that has haunted every cavity here. The island can keep it.

All that is possible, all that is up ahead. Hope fills her. She longs to be rung like a bell.

Danu is there leaning out into the sea. There is something she wants to say but Nell is not ready. A message in case she never returns. A promise to think of the island once in a while, to place a candle in the window wherever she is. For herself, for the Iníons. To bring fishermen home to the black shale curve of her back.

Out on the horizon is a ship, stout and resilient on the surf, rolling on the endless teal waves. Is it coming in or going back out? She cannot decide.

Note on Art and Artists

All of the artworks in this book are fictional, but are influenced by real artists and artworks I admire. The book's epigraph is a line from Benjamin Britten's opera *Peter Grimes*, which is carved on Maggi Hambling's *Scallop*, a sculpture on Aldeburgh beach. While Nell doesn't construct a giant scallop, shells are a feature of her beach sculptures. I've admired Hambling's wave paintings for years, and they definitely influenced how I thought and wrote about the sea, as did the waves in Wilhelmina Barns-Graham's 1988 *Sea & Boat* drawing. The carved lines and circles reference the sand art of Atsuko Tanaka, Lita Albuquerque's *Spine of the Earth* (1980) in California's Mojave Desert, Cecilia Vicuña's *Kon Kon* (2010) and Robert Smithson's *Spiral Jetty* (1970). Nell's spirals speak directly to Louise Bourgeois, who said of the spiral form: 'It has two directions. Where do you place yourself, at the periphery or at the vortex?'

The luminous boat is an homage to one of my favourite pieces of large-scale public art, *Ghost Ship* by Dorothy Cross, which was anchored off Dún Laoghaire in Dublin in 1999. Nearby is Rachel Joynt's sculpture *Mothership* (1999).

In an early draft, I included a sculpture by Nell of an ear covered in shells, inverting the idea of hearing the sea in a shell. After I had cut this, I discovered Joynt's *Mother of Pearl* (2006), and think of them as speaking to each other. Nell's self-burial performance references the *Silueta* series by Cuban-American artist Ana Mendieta, performed between 1973 and 1980. The female bible is a nod to Neva Elliott's 2004 work, *The Elliott Condensed Bible*.

The intersection of land art and politics in Beverly Buchanan's powerful *Marsh Ruins* (1981) and Agnes Denes' 1982 work *Wheatfield – A Confrontation* (where she grew a wheatfield at Battery Park in New York) are also touchstones.

I am convinced that some years back, in a park in Ireland, I heard a sound installation and have been trying to recall it ever since. Despite asking many people, I have not been able to locate the name of the artist or location. I became so immersed in Nell's process, and dreamed about her work many times and began to wonder if I hadn't imagined this work that influenced her banshee forest and beach installations. This real-or-not piece was the starting point and has something in common with Janet Cardiff's sound projects.

While writing this book, myself and composer Stephen Shannon collaborated with several artists on different projects – Alice Maher, Rachel Fallon and Aideen Barry – whose practice and exchange of ideas leave their fingerprints on this text. The durational work in the book is influenced by performance artists I've written about in the last couple of years, namely Amanda Coogan, Marina Abramović and Tehching Hsieh.

Many other artists move across these pages, so please seek out the work of Leonora Carrington, Oupa Sibeko, Carolee Schneemann, Jesse Darling, Dora Maar, Joseph Beuys, Mary Swanzy, Peter Dreher and Hilma af Klint.

This book is dedicated to the memory of another great artist: the fearless, unique and much-missed Sinéad O'Connor.

Acknowledgements

This novel was started some years before *Constellations* and in the course of its long gestation and execution, the support of many people has kept me going. I'm particularly grateful to Elaine Feeney and Louise Kennedy for their advice, laughs and friendship.

I feel lucky to have been reunited with Kishani Widyaratna as my editor. Thank you also Patrick Hargadon, Matt Clacher and all at 4th Estate.

To my agent Peter Straus, who is as fierce as he is kind, and all at RCW.

Thanks, Cormac Kinsella, for all you do, and to Patricia McVeigh and everyone at HarperCollins Ireland.

I'm extremely grateful to the Arts Council for a Next Generation Award that allowed me time away from freelance work and provided an income during lockdown to focus on writing.

To the Tyrone Guthrie Centre at Annaghmakerrig, a unique place that offers time and space to writers and artists, and hugely helped me to tune out the world and focus.

To all the artists who have informed my work and Nell's fictional world.

Thank you, Daragh Lynch of Lankum, for writing 'Danu's Libation', which is the song the Iníons sing in Chapter 73. (Buy Lankum's albums and go see them play live.)

Thank you, Neva Elliott, my best friend and constant.

To my parents, Maura and Joe, for more than I can say.

And to Stephen Shannon, Iarla and Maebh, who are the source of everything.

Danu's Libation
by Daragh Lynch

Behold, behold your blushing bride
The spitting, seething, foaming tide
The embrace of the deep black sea
Together for eternity

At death of sun and dark of year
Our harvest hymn we pray you hear
May health and bounty be our share
This gift we send to you with care

Danu, Danu hallowed mother
Take the hand of our dear brother
Fruit of earth, seed of clay
Libations on this sacred day